PONY FOR SALE

Pony for Sale

by

BERYL BYE

LUTTERWORTH PRESS

GUILDFORD AND LONDON

TO THE HORSES OF THE HEWLETT'S FARM
RIDING CENTRE, CHELTENHAM, WITH WHOM
I SPEND MANY HAPPY HOURS.

ISBN 0 7188 2194 7

PRINTED OFFSET LITHO AND BOUND IN GREAT BRITAIN
BY COX & WYMAN LTD
LONDON, FAKENHAM AND READING

Contents

Chapter 1

SOME BIG CHANGES

THE lane was too narrow for three girls and a pony to walk abreast, and anyway Candy didn't like the mud, and was so busy picking her way daintily along the dry places that she was apt to walk over everybody's feet while she was doing so. At last Cathy gave in and dropped behind, but Jane and Belinda were so busy talking that they didn't even seem to notice.

Cathy hoped that it wasn't always going to be like this—now that Belinda had come to live with Jane for three years whilst her parents were overseas. It had seemed a good idea at first, but now Cathy wasn't quite so sure. Three girls and only two ponies could be a bit awkward, she was beginning to realize that.

"I'm longing to see how Kelpie will react!" Jane was saying. "I don't think he's ever had to share his field before."

"I do hope he'll be friendly," Belinda said doubtfully. "I hope he won't kick Candy, or anything like that."

"Kelpie wouldn't kick anybody!" Cathy said indignantly. "He's the sweetest-natured pony in the world. I think he'll love having Candy to share with him. After all, he must have been lonely sometimes with no one to keep him company."

"Horses aren't like people, silly," Jane said. "They don't think and behave like people, either."

"Well, I think they do," Cathy maintained stoutly. "Kelpie does anyway. He thinks and feels and acts just like a real person, I'm sure of that."

"You sometimes talk as if Kelpie was your own pony, Cathy," Jane said a little coldly, as the procession stopped at the gate of Kelpie's field, and Belinda tried to undo the hasp with one hand and hold Candy's halter with the other. "I don't want to push the point, but remember he does belong to me. I understand Kelpie better than anyone, or ought to anyway."

Cathy went very pink as she came forward to lift the hinges of the gate for Belinda, who was still having trouble in unfastening it.

"I'm sorry, Jane," she mumbled apologetically, "It's just that . . ."

"It's just that you kidded yourself that Kelpie belonged to you when you discovered him in the field last year, and didn't know who he belonged to," Jane finished Cathy's sentence for her. "Don't think I'm not grateful. I am. After all, if it hadn't been for you I might never had plucked up the courage to start riding again after that dreadful fall. But now that I'm well again, I do think that you ought to remember that Kelpie belongs to me, and not act as if you're the only one who understands him, or knows anything about horses."

Cathy felt dreadful. She could feel a lump in her throat, and she knew if she said anything else she would burst into tears, and so she didn't answer, but just pulled the gate open in order to let Candy and the girls go through. Jane marched across the field to call Kelpie, who was grazing quietly in a far corner, but Belinda lingered behind and pressed Candy's halter into Cathy's hand.

"Hold her a moment while I shut the gate, will you, Cathy?" she asked, giving the other girl a warm and sympathetic smile.

Cathy swallowed, and taking Candy's halter she managed a weak smile in return. It was funny that it was Belinda who was being nice to her; Belinda, who used to have a reputation for being the snobbiest girl in the school.

Meanwhile Kelpie, who had been well aware of their arrival—even though he appeared not to have noticed, and had gone on cropping the lush green grass in the far corner of the field as if his life depended on it—suddenly threw up his head, and stood for all the world like one of those china horses that you can buy to stand on your mantelpiece.

Candy stopped too, and with ears well forward stared with interest towards the other pony.

"Come on, Kelpie," Jane called, "come and be introduced!" But Kelpie pretended not to hear, obviously intending to take his own time.

"I shouldn't rush him, Jane," Belinda said. "You can't hurry them into making friends. If you try and make them they'll probably loathe each other."

Cathy had been thinking along the same lines, but hadn't liked to say anything after her previous rebuff.

Candy was getting tired of waiting. She tossed her head in the air several times, making her long black mane dance upon her neck, and then began to paw the ground impatiently. Kelpie slowly began to cross the field, stopping every so often to snatch at a particularly tempting clump of grass.

"Shall I let Candy go?" Belinda asked, her hand on the halter.

"Yes, I think so," Jane agreed. "Then Kelpie won't feel we're taking sides, and trying to protect Candy or anything."

Belinda slipped off the leather and rope halter and Candy shook herself, and then stood absolutely still, watching the slowly-approaching Kelpie. Finally she began to take a few tentative steps towards the other pony, who immediately stopped as if he had done as much as common courtesy demanded, and it was now up to this trespasser to make the next move.

Candy continued to walk across the field, and Kelpie continued to watch her, until there was only a matter of six feet between the two ponies, and then Candy stopped. Kelpie extended his neck and sniffed and tentatively Candy did the same.

"Aren't they funny?" Cathy said with a giggle.

"Neither of them really wants to make the first move."

"I suppose it's up to Kelpie really," Belinda said. "It's his field."

Kelpie had advanced two steps and the ponies were now able to sniff each other nose to nose. Satisfied that Candy had the right kind of smell, Kelpie continued his tour of investigation up Candy's neck to her shoulder, and then, having apparently made up his mind, he put out his tongue and gently began to lick the little mare's neck.

"He likes her," Cathy breathed. "I knew he would."

"He's got a funny way of showing it," Belinda said doubtfully, as Kelpie took a sudden nip at Candy's flank, and the mare began a spirited canter around the field with Kelpie in hot pursuit.

"They're only playing," Jane said confidently "look! they've stopped now, and Kelpie is licking her again. I don't think we've got anything to worry about. You can hang that halter in the shed, Belinda," Jane went on. "It saves lugging it backwards and forwards from the house every time. I shall have to get Dad to enlarge the shed a bit. It's not really big enough for two ponies."

The girls began to walk across the field to the rough log cabin which had been made of split pines from the little plantation that grew close by.

Cathy remembered her first sight of it over a year ago, when she had discovered Kelpie's saddle and bridle, lying dirty and unused in the

corner, and had given in to the temptation to ride
the scruffy little pony with the white blaze, who
didn't seem to belong to anybody. She hadn't
known Jane then, Jane, who was the pony's rightful
owner, but who lay paralysed at the Farm not far
away, suffering from the effects of a riding accident
from which she seemed unlikely to recover. But
Jane had recovered, and had now taken full possession of her pony again, and although Cathy was, of
course, very happy about this, Jane was making it
quite clear that things would be on a different
footing now.

"I can't really believe that you're going to live
with us for three whole years," Jane was saying
to Belinda, when Cathy came out of her little
reverie.

"Well, it won't really be for a whole three
years," Belinda pointed out, "I shall be going out
to Hong Kong to stay with Mummy and Daddy at
Christmas, and in the summer. That will take quite
a chunk out of it."

"Well, nearly three years," Jane amended.
"Not counting the holidays. It will be funny going
to school too, instead of having lessons with Miss
Beckford."

"She's not Miss Beckford now," Cathy reminded her. "What do you call her, anyway?"

"I don't call her anything," Jane confessed. "I
can't call her Miss Beckford now that she's my
stepmother, and somehow it sounds silly to call
her Mother, when she's not."

"I think stepmother is a horrid word," Belinda said. "I always think of Cinderella, or the Babes in the Wood, or something like that."

"Oh, she's not as bad as that," Jane confessed. "It's just that when someone has been your governess for the last three years, it comes as a bit of a shock when your father suddenly ups and marries her!"

"He must have been very lonely," Cathy said quietly. "All those years without your mother, especially when you were ill as well."

"And now we've all got company," Jane said briskly. "Dad's got Miss Beckford, Kelpie's got Candy, and I've got Belinda—a grown-up, ready-made sister, so no one need be lonely any more."

Cathy thought of Jane's words later that evening as she walked down the hill from Monk's Coombe.

"Dad's got Miss Beckford, Kelpie's got Candy, and I've got Belinda—" It seemed as if that was how it was going to be from now on, she thought sadly. Once Jane had been her friend, and so had Belinda, but now that they had each other they didn't seem to need her any more. Two ponies between three wasn't going to work out very well either. Cathy could tell that. Oh, Jane and Belinda would let her have the odd ride she was sure, but she would always feel awkward about it, knowing that it meant that one of them must stay at home. Cathy felt the old rebellion stirring inside her. It wasn't fair. Why should Jane and Belinda be lucky enough to own ponies, while she, Cathy—who loved horses more than either of them—should have to be content with just an occasional ride. Almost she wished that Jane hadn't got better, or not so quickly anyway, and then she hated herself for having such wicked thoughts.

"Forgive me, God!" she whispered to herself. "I didn't really mean it. Of course I'm glad that Jane is better, and please help me not to get mean and bitter about Jane and Belinda, so that the way I behave may make them want to know more about You."

Thinking about God made Cathy think about Joy. She had forgotten that Joy was coming to stay with them! That would be fun! Cathy hadn't seen Joy since the Youth Camp that they had both attended where Cathy had first become a follower of the Lord Jesus, and promised to give her life into His keeping. Now, Joy was going out to Africa to be a missionary, and she was coming to stay with Cathy and her parents for a few days before she sailed.

When Cathy arrived home she found her mother in the kitchen, and the warm spicy smell that filled the air made Cathy suddenly feel hungry.

"I've got Joy's room ready," Mrs. Smith said, "and I've made up the bed. I thought you might like to pick some roses from the garden and put a vase upstairs. It always looks welcoming to put flowers in a room."

The roses were the first thing that Joy noticed when Cathy took her up to her room the following morning.

"My favourite flower!" she said as she bent over them and sniffed at their sweet scent. "I think I shall miss them more than any other flower when I'm in Africa."

"Are you sorry to be going?" Cathy asked, sitting down on the end of Joy's bed, and twisting the fringe of the candlewick bedspread between her fingers.

"I'm all mixed up about it really," Joy confessed. "Of course I shall be sad to leave England, and my parents, and all my friends. And it's frightening going to a strange country to work, where you don't know anybody and you don't know what it will be like. But in another way I'm glad—because I think this is what God wants me to do. And if we're in the right place doing the right job, then that's the only way we can be sure of being really happy."

"You said 'I think this is what God wants me to do'," Cathy said thoughtfully. "Aren't you sure?"

Joy moved over to the window and stood looking out, but somehow Cathy didn't think she was really seing the neat little garden with its green lawn edged with flower beds, but was staring right through it as if she was seeing something that lay far beyond.

"It's funny you should ask that, Cathy," she

answered at last, "because being absolutely sure
has been one of the very hardest things I've ever
had to decide. But I am sure now—at least I
think so, but if it's not right for me to go to Africa,
then I hope God will show me before it's too
late."

Joy came and sat down on the bed beside
Cathy.

"It's funny talking to you like this," she said,
smiling down on the younger girl, "it's usually
you telling me things, isn't it, instead of me telling
you. But I did have a hard time trying to find out
if I should go to Africa or not, and it was strange
the way you asked me about it just now, just as if
you knew all about it."

'When I went for my first interview to the
Missionary Society I was turned down," Joy went
on. "It was a great disappointment because you
see I thought they'd jump at me, a young, keen
teacher with very clear Christian ideals who was
prepared to go absolutely anywhere where there
was a need. But they didn't jump at me at all. They
told me to go away and do a year's theological
training and then come back again, and that's what
I did."

"And that was why you went to College?"
Cathy said.

"Yes, I had a lot to learn about the Bible," Joy
said. "I thought I knew it all until I went to College
and after the first month I began to think I didn't
know anything at all."

"And what did you do when the year was over?" Cathy asked curiously.

"I went back to the Missionary Society again," Joy said.

"And—?" Cathy pressed.

"And—" Joy said. "They turned me down again."

"But why?" Cathy asked in amazement.

"They said they weren't sure that it was God's Will that I should go to Kuampuala as a teacher at this time," Joy said with a sigh. "They said that the situation was changing every day and getting more difficult, and it was doubtful if the Government would allow any more Christian missionaries into the country, even if they did have special qualifications. They told me to take a job for a year in England, and then come back again."

"But you didn't," Cathy remarked.

"No," Joy said, "I still felt that God wanted me to go out there, and to go at once. So I decided to go out independently. My godfather died two years ago and left me several hundred pounds. Enough to fit me out with tropical clothing and to pay my fare. I've got an uncle who is a lecturer at a University near Kuampuala, and he arranged the teaching post for me. I shall be able to live with him at first too. So you see, I was able to get things fixed up quite quickly in the end."

"I think you're awfully brave," Cathy said admiringly.

"I don't feel brave at all," Joy confessed, "I'm

terrified inside. I do hope I'm doing the right thing. It's so terribly hard to be absolutely sure. And now let's talk about you," Joy said, suddenly changing the subject.

Chapter 2

JOINING THE PONY CLUB

"I HOPE I shall be able to meet Jane and Belinda and to see this marvellous Kelpie that I've heard so much about," Joy said, as she and Cathy, were washing the breakfast dishes the following morning. "And the other pony, 'Sugar' I think you said she was called."

"Candy," Cathy corrected. "Of course things are different now, Belinda has gone to live with the Parminters because her parents have gone abroad, and Miss Beckford, that's the governess, has married the Major, and so Jane has got a step-mother."

"And do you still ride?" Joy enquired.

"Oh, yes!" Cathy said. "But not so often of course. You see now that Jane is better she mostly rides Kelpie herself."

There was a short pause.

"I see," Joy said gently. "And you find that rather hard, and sometimes I expect you wish, just a little, that Jane hadn't got better quite so quickly."

"Oh, Joy, how did you guess?" Cathy said, flushing pinkly with embarrassment.

"Because I expect it's just the way I would feel in the same circumstances," Joy said dryly.

"Oh, I'm sure you wouldn't," Cathy denied

hotly. "You're not as horrid as I am. You'd be glad about Jane and be pleased that she was fit, and able to ride her own pony again."

"I do wish that you'd realize that I'm no different to anyone else," Joy said, smiling down at her young friend with twinkling eyes. "Sometimes I'm quite thankful that only God really knows what we're like inside, and sometimes I'm absolutely ashamed at what He must see when He looks into my heart. It's so easy to appear nice outside you know, particularly if no one gives you anything to be nasty about!"

"I *am* glad about Jane really," Cathy said firmly, "it's just sometimes that I get these nasty thoughts. But I do know they're wicked and wrong, and I do remember to say a quick prayer asking for forgiveness, and God does seem to answer it."

"Then you've made a big step forwards," Joy said. "Sometimes it takes Christians a whole lifetime to learn to do just that. If only we can talk to Him at any time and about anything, then we have learned the most important thing in the Christian life."

The four days that Joy spent with the Smith family went very quickly. Cathy took her up to the farm and introduced her to Kelpie, and Miss Beckford—or Mrs. Parminter as Cathy was learning to call her—invited them both to tea which was great fun. Afterwards Jane and Belinda and Cathy saddled up the ponies and Jane insisted that Joy should have a ride.

"You'll probably have to ride in Africa," she pointed out, "so you might as well have some practice while you've got the chance!"

Jane was a very good teacher and Joy did exactly as she was told, and so it wasn't long before she was trotting around the field on Kelpie, and looking remarkably comfortable.

"You must come again tomorrow," Jane said. "You've done very well for a first lesson."

"Thank you for those few kind words, Miss Parminter," Joy laughed, "but I think I have used muscles today that I never even knew I possessed. By this time tomorrow I shall probably be so stiff that I shan't be able to get out of bed, and you and Kelpie will have to visit me with your very best bedside manner."

"Nonsense," Jane said briskly. "If you're stiff you will just have to get loosened up again with some more riding.'

"She's a terrible bully," Cathy informed Joy. "I remember how she used to go on at me when she was teaching me to jump!"

"They're nice girls, Cathy," Joy said as they were on their way home from the farm. "But Belinda isn't a bit as I expected."

"She's changed a lot," Cathy said quickly. "She's quite a different person from what she used to be."

"Does she still come to Bible Class?" Joy wanted to know.

"Well, she did," Cathy said. "But we have broken up for the summer, you see, and when we start again in September I wonder if she'll find it's too far to come. I haven't asked Jane about it yet, either."

"Wouldn't Major Parminter run them down in the car?" Joy asked.

"Well, I think he would," Cathy said. "That is if they really wanted to come. But if they didn't they could make that an excuse, if you see what I mean."

"Yes, I do," Joy said. "But it's something we could pray about. That Belinda should really want to come and should encourage Jane to come with her."

"It's so hard to find the right time to mention it," Cathy confessed. "When we're together we're always talking about horses, and riding, and jumping and gymkhanas and all that. It never seems to be the right time to talk about God and Bible Class."

"I know what you mean," Joy agreed, "and I think it's very important to choose the right moment for something like that. But if you are really alert, Cathy, and looking for your opportunity, then I'm sure that just the right moment will turn up."

"I wish you weren't going away, Joy," Cathy said suddenly, smiling at her friend rather wistfully.

"But you'll still be able to write to me, Cathy," Joy pointed out cheerfully. "And three years isn't very long. In three years I shall be coming home

on my first leave, and think how much I shall have
to tell you."

Cathy thought of Joy's words as she stood on the
platform of Bedborough station the following Saturday, sadly waving Joy's train out of sight. "Three
years isn't very long," Joy had said. But neither
Joy nor Cathy realized that it would be considerably
less than three years before they would see each
other again.

That afternoon, when Cathy went up to the farm
to see her friends, she found that Jane had had one
of her "good ideas" and was trying to persuade
her father to agree to her plan.

"Just think of the time that it will save you,
Daddy!" Jane pointed out, as if consideration for
her father was the main purpose of the idea.
"Otherwise you'll have to take Belinda and me
down to school in the morning, and then come back,
and then come down again in the afternoon and
back again, that will mean four journeys a day,
and it will take you ages, and I don't know how
much petrol!"

"And of course that is what is really troubling
you?" Major Parminter said, with a twinkle in his
eye. "The thought of me getting exhausted ferry-
ing you backwards and forwards, and the huge
sums of money that I shall have to spend on
petrol!"

"Well, it's not ONLY that," Jane confessed, "but
it does come into it, doesn't it? I mean, of course
Belinda and I would enjoy riding Kelpie and Candy

to school, but it would make it easier for you AS WELL, wouldn't it?"

"And what would you do with the ponies during the day?" the Major wanted to know. "I suppose you've got that all fixed up as well."

"Oh, yes," Jane said. "We could leave them at Mr. Styles' stable during the day. It's not far from school, and Cathy says they've got a tack room there where we could change our jodhpurs for skirts."

"You've certainly got it all worked out," her father said thoughtfully. "But what about the huge sums of money that I should have to pay Mr. Styles for the hay that the ponies would eat during the day?"

"Oh, Daddy, you're just teasing," Jane said in exasperation. "The ponies wouldn't eat any more at the stables then they would at home."

"The ponies would be turned out if they were at home," The Major pointed out.

"But can we. . . .?" Jane persisted. "That's what I want to know."

Mrs. Parminter, who was sitting by the fire knitting a school sweater for Jane, and who until then had had nothing to say, suddenly spoke.

"I don't see why the children shouldn't ride their ponies to school, John," she said. "It would give all four of them some regular exercise, and providing Mr. Styles would be prepared to keep them during the day, it might work out rather well. Of course we'd still have to take them in the car if the weather was unsuitable. I should think that Harp Hill would be terribly dangerous for a pony if it were at all icy."

"Oh, thank you, Mother," Jane used the word for the first time to her new stepmother without really realizing it.

"Then it will be all right, Daddy?" she pressed, determined to get everything firmly settled without any doubts.

"If your mother thinks so," Major Parminter said at last. "And providing Mr. Styles agrees."

School started the following Monday. The girls arrived at the stables, unsaddled the ponies and then changed into their school skirts behind a partition in the tack room.

Cathy rushed up as they entered the school playground, and wanted to know if everything had worked out all right.

"It was super fun," Jane said. "Belinda put on her skirt on top of her jodhpurs, and then nearly forgot to take them off from underneath. She did look funny. Is there somewhere we can have a wash? I feel all horsy."

"Lucky things," Cathy thought to herself as she led the way to the cloakrooms. And then she remembered the verses of the Bible that she had been reading that morning with the help of her Notes.

"Thou shalt not covet thy neighbour's house, thou shalt not covet thy neighbour's wife, nor his manservant, nor his maidservant, nor his ox, nor his ass, nor anything that is thy neighbour's."

She had been rather amused as she read through the list. She had no need to covet her neighbour's house, because it was exactly the same as their own. She certainly didn't covet her neighbour's wife because old Mr. Hall's wife was very old, very deaf, very ugly and very cross! Neither Mrs. Hall nor Mrs Martin (who lived the other side) had any help in the house, so manservants and maidservants didn't come into it either, and the thought of Mr. Martin leading an ox or a donkey out to feed on his precious back lawn had given Cathy the giggles. It was the last bit of the verse that had stuck in Cathy's mind, and it was these words that she thought of now. . . . .

"Nor *anything* that is thy neighbour's."

"Anything" was ponies in general and Kelpie in particular, and the fact that Jane lived on Harp Hill and not actually next door to Cathy didn't make the slightest difference.

"Please, please, God, help me not to be jealous," Cathy prayed suddenly. "I know I shouldn't. But O God, it is so very hard."

"Have you got something in your eye, Cathy?" Belinda asked with concern, and the question made Cathy realize that she must have screwed up her eyes as she was saying her little prayer.

"Oh! No-o," Cathy replied, knowing that the girls would think it very funny if they knew why she had her eyes closed at that particular moment.

"Let's take Jane to our formroom," Belinda said,

"I suppose we'll be in Class Three now that we've moved up.

"Thank goodness Lampry has left," Cathy said thankfully. "I wonder what the new teacher will be like."

The new teacher's name turned out to be Miss Bright, and she was tall and fair with short curly hair and a mouth that seemed to be made in the right shape for laughing. She was dressed in a pale blue suit with a neat turned down collar, and on the lapel of her suit was pinned a little badge. Cathy stared and stared, and could hardly believe her eyes, for the badge that Miss Bright was wearing was the same shape as the one that was printed on the cover of the Bible Notes that Cathy had been reading that very morning.

"I shall try to learn five different names each day," Miss Bright was saying," and so, by next week, I ought to know you all. In the meantime you'll have to forgive me if I say 'You in the back seat' or 'you with the pink cheeks' when I don't know your name!"

As the girls sat on their desks munching their biscuits at breaktime, Jane mentioned an idea to Cathy and Belinda that had been in her mind for some time.

"I vote we join the Pony Club," she said. "I've been meaning to for a long time, but somehow it didn't seem worth it when I was ill. But now there's three of us, I think we could have some fun."

"I can't join," Cathy said sadly, "Remember I haven't got a pony."

"That doesn't matter," Jane said at once. "You don't have to actually own a pony before you can belong. As long as you love horses and like riding, that's all that matters."

"But I couldn't go to any of the meetings with you if I had to go on foot," Cathy pointed out.

"You could borrow one of Mr. Styles' ponies," Jane suggested.

"Or take turns in riding ours," Belinda put in.

"I don't think Mummy and Daddy could afford to let me hire a pony for a whole day," Cathy said. sadly. "And it would spoil it for you if we had to share."

"You're just making difficulties," Jane said crossly. "The first thing to do is to join the Pony Club. We can sort out afterwards what we are going to do about the riding side of it."

"You are bossy, Jane," Belinda said a little admiringly. "You always get so mad if people won't do exactly as you say!"

"I just get angry when people make excuses," Jane said crisply. "And try to make things seem difficult when really they're as easy as pie."

Once Jane made up her mind about something there was no stopping her, and by the end of the week she had not only obtained the forms from the local Secretary, but had insisted on Belinda and Cathy completing theirs, and had posted the three away. A week later their badges and membership

cards arrived, together with a list of the local events
that had been arranged for the next six months.

"There's a Treasure Hunt next week," Jane said,
as the girls were poring over the list while balanced
precariously on the gate of the ponies' field on the
following Saturday.

"Where is it to be held?" Cathy asked, trying to
lean over and read the notice without falling off the
gate.

"Barton Travers," Jane said. "That's not too
far away."

'I wonder what you do?" Belinda wanted to
know.

"I suppose you have clues and things," Jane
said. "And you have to go from one point to the
next as quickly as possible. That's what you do in
an ordinary Treasure Hunt anyway."

"Who is going to ride?" Belinda asked thoughtfully. "We said we'd share the ponies if Cathy
belonged."

"Well," Jane said, "we normally would of
course. But as this is the first thing we're going to,
I think it's only fair that we ride Kelpie and Candy.
After that it will be different."

"That's a bit hard on Cathy," Belinda pointed
out doubtfully.

"I don't mind," Cathy said quickly, and completely untruthfully. "You go, and then you can
tell me all about it. After all, I did know that I
wouldn't always be able to go to things as I haven't
got a pony. And perhaps I'll be able to save up and

hire one of Mr. Styles' ponies for the next time. I talked to Mummy and Daddy about it, and they said they'd help."

"Well, if you're sure you don't mind," Belinda said with obvious relief, and Cathy knew she would have felt just the same if she were Belinda.

Chapter 3

A NEW FRIEND

THE next three weeks passed very quickly for the girls. Now that school had started again there was little time for riding, except at the weekends, and Cathy usually managed to spend part of Saturday at the farm. She had mentioned to Jane and Belinda about the Bible Class, it started again in September, and Jane had argued about it quite a lot before she finally agreed to come.

"I'm only going to try it though," she said the first time Cathy mentioned it. "If I find that it's awfully boring or a complete waste of time, then I shall pack it in."

"It's not boring," Belinda said. "At least I don't think so anyway. We have quizzes and competitions and things, and the leader always makes the talks interesting, as if she's talking about things that really happened, and not just making them up."

"But they did really happen," Cathy pointed out. "That's what's so exciting about the Bible. It's about real people doing real things. Ordinary people like you and me."

"But people in the Bible were always good!" Jane argued.

"They weren't!" Cathy said. "Some of them

were downright wicked, and did much worse things than you or me."

"Well, who for instance?" Jane wanted to know.

"The Israelite people for one," Cathy said. "They did nothing but moan the whole time that they were slaves in Egypt, and then when God arranged to set them free, and give them a land of their own, they grumbled and complained every step of the way. First they complained about the food. They said that everything was much better in Egypt, and they wished they could go back there."

"Well, I should have told them to jolly well go," Jane said indignantly.

"But God's not like that," Cathy said. "He doesn't throw you over just because He gets fed up with you. If He did, He'd have finished with me long ago."

"I wish you wouldn't always speak as if God's a special personal kind of friend," Jane complained.

"But He is," Cathy insisted. "That's what I'm always trying to make you understand. You thought of Him like that once, Jane. When you wanted Him to help you walk again, do you remember?"

Jane looked a little uncomfortable, and for once couldn't think of any answer, so Cathy ventured to go on.

"My mother says that friendships have to be kept in good repair," she said quietly.

"And what does she mean by that?" Jane wanted to know.

"She means that if you want to keep a friendship then you've got to keep it mended, otherwise it falls apart like a piece of material that no one bothers to look after. If I don't write to Joy for instance, or if I never bothered to meet you and Belinda, and talk to you and listen to what you've got to say, then we soon wouldn't be friends any more. Not real friends anyway."

"I don't know how this started," Jane said a trifle crossly. "Who was talking about friendship anyway?"

"You were," Cathy reminded her. "You said you didn't like me speaking of God as if He was a special kind of friend."

"And Cathy said you thought of Him like that once," Belinda finished.

"What I was trying to say," Cathy said, "was that if you don't keep your friendship with God 'in repair', then it will fall apart. That is why it is a good thing to read your Bible, and go to Church and to the Bible Class on Sunday afternoon."

"And that's where all this started," Belinda said patiently. "With you coming to Bible Class on Sunday afternoon."

"What about riding?" Jane said, feeling as she was being cornered into doing something against her will, and looking for a way out.

Cathy knew that the question of riding would come up sooner or later, so she was ready for it.

"Bible Class comes first on a Sunday," she said firmly. "For me anyway. It doesn't seem fair otherwise, if you only bother about God if you've nothing better to do." And they left it at that.

The following Sunday both Jane and Belinda came to Bible Class and Cathy was delighted. She wasn't much good at praying regularly for anything or anyone. She remembered for the first two or three times, and then if God hadn't answered she got fed up, and gradually she forgot all about it. But Joy and she had a private agreement about Jane and Belinda, and Joy had given her a special note book while she was staying with Cathy, and Cathy had written JANE AND BELINDA— BIBLE CLASS in black ink on the first line. Because Cathy knew that Joy was praying as well, she felt they had entered into a kind of pact, and she didn't want to let Joy down by forgetting to pray.

"Don't just pray—'Please let Belinda and Jane come to the Bible Class' and then forget about it," Joy had said. "Pray 'Please let Jane and Belinda come next Sunday', and pray that every week, then you will be able to see how God answers your prayer."

Cathy had followed Joy's advice, and by the end of September she had prayed for three weeks and Jane and Belinda had come for three weeks, so Cathy felt quite pleased with herself, with Jane and Belinda and with God. She had also written a second line underneath JANE AND BELINDA in her notebook. It was just two words ME and JEALOUSY, and that was a prayer that Cathy found she needed to pray every single day, for not only did she find it very hard not to be jealous of Jane and Belinda being friends, but she found it even harder not be jealous of Kelpie and Candy, and the way that the friends could ride whenever they liked.

On the Saturday of the Treasure Hunt, Cathy went up to the farm to help Jane and Belinda get the ponies ready. Not that the girls really needed any help, but Cathy couldn't resist seeing them set off anyway, even if she couldn't go herself.

"I wish you were coming Cathy," Belinda said as she and Cathy checked the girths before mounting. "It won't be half as much fun without you."

Cathy could never understand why it was that when someone said something kind to you, if you were feeling unhappy, it nearly always made you want to cry.

"You'll be able to tell me all about it," Cathy said gruffly. "And perhaps next time I'll be able to go."

She watched her friends trot off down the road, their macintoshes bouncing merrily on their saddles, and then she sighed a really big sigh, and started to walk slowly across the fields to the short cut that led through the gorse bushes down to the town.

Cathy was so deep in her own thoughts that she didn't notice the tall slim figure in brown and a yellow polo-neck sweater who was walking briskly up the hill path as Cathy was coming down. It wasn't until they were nearly face to face that Cathy looked up.

"It's Cathy Smith, isn't it?" the lady said, wrinkling her forehead in thought. "I didn't expect to find you up here on your own. I always think of you as 'the trio'. Where are the others?"

"They've gone to a Pony Club Treasure Hunt," Cathy told her. "I've been to see them off."

"Why haven't you gone as well?" Miss Bright wanted to know.

"I haven't got a pony of my own," Cathy said sadly. "They let me ride Kelpie or Candy sometimes, but this was the first Treasure Hunt they've been to, so of course they wanted to ride."

"I see," Miss Bright said. "So it's left you at rather a loose end?"

"Yes," Cathy said, and then somehow she couldn't think of anything else to say.

"I've been meaning to find out about riding," Miss Bright suddenly broke the silence. "I used to ride before I went to University, and then there was so much to do that I let it drop. Do you happen to know if there is anywhere in Bedborough where you can hire horses? Where they will let you take a horse out by yourself?"

"There's Mr. Styles," Cathy said quickly. "That's the stable where Jane and Belinda leave their ponies when they come to school."

"Where is that?" Miss Bright wanted to know.

"I could show you," Cathy said eagerly. "I haven't really got anything else to do."

"I would be glad if you would," Miss Bright said. "It's so much easier to be shown than to try and follow someone else's directions. Let's go now," she went on. "Otherwise I shall keep putting it off and never get round to doing anything about it."

Mr. Styles was quite willing for Miss Bright to take one of his horses out when he realized that she was an accomplished rider, in fact he suggested that she took advantage of the lovely afternoon, and went for a ride there and then.

"Why not?" Miss Bright agreed. "And I shall take Cathy with me to show me the best rides and to keep me company."

"But I haven't—" Cathy began rather awkwardly.

"Oh, it's my treat," Miss Bright said. "A sort of thank-you for introducing me to Mr. Styles and making me really do something about taking up riding again, instead of just thinking about it."

Cathy's spirits soared as they trotted out of the stable yard and turned their horses towards the hills. What a lovely and unexpected treat, just when she'd been feeling down in the dumps and thoroughly fed up.

Miss Bright was very easy to talk to, and it wasn't long before Cathy found herself telling the teacher all about Kelpie, and Jane's fall and the circumstances which followed it. She told her about Joy too, and how her friend had gone out to Africa to be a missionary.

"I wanted to be a missionary too," Miss Bright said quietly, "but somehow it seems as if God has shut the door. For the time being anyway. I've come to live with my brother in Bedborough," she went on. "He is married to a very sweet girl and they've got two adorable little boys. But a few months ago Kay—that's my sister-in-law—slipped on the stairs and hurt her back, and now she's in a plaster jacket, and life is a bit difficult for her with such an active family. That's why I applied for a job in Bedborough. I thought if I lived with them it would be easier to help."

"Is she getting better?" Cathy asked with concern.

"Yes, she is," Miss Bright said thankfully. "But I think it will be rather a long job."

"I want your sister-in-law to get better," Cathy said, "but I hope you'll be here for a long time."

"That's nice of you," Miss Bright laughed. "I hope you still think so when we tackle those decimal sums on Monday, and you keep forgetting where to put the point! And now let's have a canter," she said briskly. "These horses are just longing to get rid of some of their energy."

"Did you have a rotten time?" was Belinda's first question when they met for Bible Class the following day.

"No, it was super!" Cathy told her. "Wait until afterwards and I'll tell you all about it."

It wasn't until halfway through the first hymn

that Cathy remembered she had completely forgotten to question her friend about the Treasure Hunt!

On the following Monday Cathy received a letter from Joy. Cathy loved having letters, but she was learning that if you wanted to receive letters, then you had to write them, and as she wasn't very fond of writing letters, it wasn't often that the postman delivered anything that was of special interest to her! Cathy didn't know very much about Africa in general, or Kuampuala in particular, but she had imagined that it must be very exciting going out to work in a foreign country where the sun was always shining and there were plenty of horses to ride.

"It's terribly hot here," Joy wrote. "In fact the only time that I feel really cool is when I am actually standing under a cool shower, but I am afraid the effects of that soon wears off. I seem to spend half of the day showering and changing my clothes. I am staying with my uncle at the moment. I had hoped to get a small flat near the school where I am working, but my uncle does not think it would be wise for me to live alone at the moment, as some of the African people do not feel very friendly towards white people, and sometimes quite fierce fighting breaks out over some small matter, and the police have to be called to break it up. The children in my class are very sweet. They do not seem to feel the heat at all, and tear around the compound (as they call the playground) at playtime, just like English children do at home. I have been to tea at the Mission in Kuampuala and everyone was very kind and friendly. The missionaries are all doing some sort of job in the town. There are doctors and nurses, teachers and even what we would call 'civil servants'—people who are helping the country to run it's business affairs.

"DO PLEASE PRAY FOR ME CATHY." (Joy had written the words in big capital letters). "People think that because you are a missionary you are a 'better than ordinary' person, and this is just not true. It is so hot here that it makes one feel very lazy and it is a very great temptation not to bother about reading my Bible, or praying, but just to lie down in a long cane chair with a cold drink, whenever I get the chance! Sometimes I feel much further away from God than I did when I was in England, and this frightens me a little, so pray that I may always know He is with me, and that He will strengthen and guide me every day."

Cathy had taken the letter up to her bedroom to read. Grown-ups' writing wasn't always very easy to understand, and Joy was almost grown up and her writing was a bit squiggley and sloping. But there was no misunderstanding the capitals DO PLEASE PRAY FOR ME, and they reminded Cathy about her prayer notebook in her Bible, and so she took it out and wrote the name 'JOY' underneath 'JANE AND BELINDA' and 'ME' and 'JEALOUSY', which were the first three entries in her book. She really felt that she was getting somewhere these days. Jane and Belinda were coming to Bible Class regularly, and she hadn't been jealous over Kelpie for two whole days! Of course it would be her turn to ride the pony on Saturday, she admitted to herself, and so perhaps she hadn't quite as much cause to be jealous as she usually had! And now she must pray about Joy—every day—just as she was slowly learning to pray about other things.

Cathy did hope that Joy was happy. She sat down and read the letter again. There was really nothing in it that sounded as if she was—UN-happy—but that wasn't quite the same thing. She put the letter away and went to get ready for school.

Chapter 4

WHAT HAPPENED TO KELPIE

AT break, Cathy, Jane and Belinda sat on the climbing apparatus, swinging their legs and talking.

"The Pony Club have a paper chase on Sunday," Jane said. "I bet it will be super fun."

"It's your turn to ride, isn't it, Jane?" Belinda said. "You and Cathy are taking the ponies to be shod on Saturday, so it will be you and me riding the ponies the next day. It's a pity we haven't got three ponies, so that we could all go."

"What about Bible Class?" Cathy said in a small voice.

There was an awkward silence.

"Well," Jane said, "We can go to Bible Class every Sunday, but the paper chase only happens about once a year."

"I don't see that makes any difference," Cathy said stubbornly. "I thought we sorted that out weeks ago."

"You did," Jane said. "I didn't say anything about it. What about you, Belinda?"

Belinda shifted uncomfortably on the bars. "I don't know," she said at last.

"But you must know!" Jane said briskly. "You've got to make up your mind. Are you coming to the paper chase with me, or are you going to be a goody-goody and stay home and go to the Bible Class with Cathy? It's as simple as that!"

For a moment Belinda didn't answer, and Cathy hoped so much that her friend would stand firmly at her side, but before she could answer Jane spoke again.

"After all," she said, "it doesn't really matter as far as Cathy is concerned. It's not as if it's her turn to ride anyway."

"I suppose not," Belinda said at last. "I don't really want to miss the paper chase," she said reluctantly. "Would you mind terribly, Cathy, if I didn't go just this once?"

"You must make up your own mind," Cathy said, trying to sound as if she didn't care either way. "I don't want to force you to go."

"It's only this once," Belinda said, slipping her hand through Cathy's arm and giving it a squeeze.

"Then that's settled," Jane said firmly, jumping down off the apparatus and dusting her hands. "I think they use sawdust and not paper, even though it's called a 'Paper Chase'. It's not so untidy, you see."

Belinda and Jane were tactful enough not to discuss the paper chase in front of Cathy again, and it wasn't until Sunday afternoon, when Cathy was getting ready for Bible Class, that she remembered the event and realized that her friends wouldn't be present at the meeting.

She hadn't expected to see her friends again until the following day, and so she was very surprised to see Belinda, looking very worried and untidy, struggling with the latch on the gate at five o'clock that evening.

"It's Belinda," Cathy said to her mother in surprise. "I wonder what she wants?"

Cathy was waiting at the door for her friend as she came up the front path, and was concerned to see how upset Belinda looked.

"Whatever is the matter?" Cathy burst out before her friend had a chance to say anything.

"It's Kelpie," Belinda said, and Cathy could tell she was on the verge of tears. "He's hurt."

"Hurt?" Cathy said sharply. "How?"

Mrs. Smith had come to the door where the two friends were still standing.

"I should bring Belinda in," she said gently, "and then she can tell you all about it."

"It was at the gate," Belinda said in a choking voice. "We couldn't all get through."

"What gate?" Cathy asked. "Where did it happen?"

"Perhaps if you started at the beginning," Mrs. Smith suggested quietly.

"Yes," Belinda said with a gulp. "Of course. We all met at Stamford Cross on the village green. It's about a mile away. You know, where the hounds meet sometimes. The party who were laying the trail had left about twenty minutes before, so as to give them plenty of time to get ahead. Then a horn was blown by the Club Secretary, and that was the signal for everyone to set off. It didn't take long to find the trail because once one person saw it, they yelled out, and so everyone charged off in the same direction. Only of course, the best ponies got in front because they could go faster you see. Then we came to a fence and we could see that the trail went over it. Some of the bigger riders decided to jump it, so it was all right for them. Jane wanted to jump it too, but it was quite high and the landing was a bit tricky, so I persuaded her to come round with me to the gate. A lot of the smaller children had found it already." Belinda paused for breath.

"And then?" Cathy pressed.

"This meant that we got rather behind," Belinda said. "You know what Jane is like. She doesn't like being behind in anything. So she shouted to me to gallop on so that we could catch up the leaders. Candy and Kelpie were as excited as the rest by this time and the trail led over this nice flat field so we were simply whizzing along, and the leaders weren't very far ahead. Kelpie had got his tail streaming out like a banner, and was thoroughly enjoying himself and then we saw the gateway ahead."

"And what happened?" Cathy said, almost dancing with impatience.

"The gate was open," Belinda said, "And Jane was only a few yards behind the leaders. Kelpie seemed to give a little surge forward and then it happened."

"What happened?" Cathy demanded. "For goodness sake tell me."

"The gate was open," Belinda said. "But one of the bigger horses that was in the lead seemed to kick out sideways at Kelpie just as he was drawing level. He caught Kelpie on the knee."

"Oh—no," Cathy said, burying her face in her hands.

"Yes," Belinda said. "And Kelpie sort of collapsed. Luckily Jane managed to roll clear and she wasn't hurt at all."

"That was a good thing," Mrs. Smith said "After her last fall it would have been a bad thing if Jane had been hurt again."

"But what about Kelpie?" Cathy said, and was horrified to realize that she cared more about the pony than Jane at that moment.

"He scrambled to his feet," Belinda said, "and stood there trembling and looking sort of ashamed, as if it was all his fault. It was terrible," Belinda said, beginning to cry, "I felt so sorry for him. He kept his knee bent, and every so often he put his nose down and touched it as if it hurt dreadfully."

"But he got kicked before," Cathy said. "You know, at the gymkhana when I borrowed him without asking. He got better then."

"Oh, this was much, much worse," Belinda insisted. "And the vet said that knee injuries are very, very tricky. And he couldn't promise that he'd ever be absolutely well."

"The vet?" Cathy said. "How was it the vet was there?"

"He wasn't at first," Belinda explained. "Everyone was ever so kind. In fact, they forgot about the paper chase and all gathered round to help. There was a cottage quite near, and luckily they had the phone on, so Jane went and telephoned her father, and he came over in the Land Rover. He had a look at Kelpie and then said he didn't think he ought to walk on his leg at all. Not until the vet had seen it anyway. And one of the pony club members had a horse box at home, and she went back with the Major in his car to fetch it. We got Kelpie back to the Farm eventually, and the Major phoned for the vet. Oh, Cathy, it was awful. Like somebody dying or something."

"But Kelpie isn't dead?" Cathy said unbelievingly, hardly daring to ask the question.

"No, of course he isn't," Belinda said. "But it's almost as bad for a horse, isn't it? Not knowing if he'll ever be able to walk properly again, or be ridden or anything."

"Is it really as bad as that?" Cathy said slowly.

"That's why I wanted to come and tell you," Belinda said. "I know you love Kelpie better than any of us. And I thought you'd want to know at once that he was injured. Oh, if only we hadn't gone on that stupid paper chase," Belinda wailed. "This dreadful accident would never have happened."

"Now, Belinda," Mrs. Smith said firmly, "you can't possibly blame yourself for what has happened. It was just an accident, and if it hadn't happened today it could equally well have happened some other time. You must realize that. I expect you want to go and have a look at Kelpie," Cathy's mother turned to her daughter. "So go and put on a thick sweater and your wellingtons, while I give Belinda a hot drink. I am sure she can do with it."

"Oh, no, I don't want anything, thank you," Belinda said, but Mrs. Smith wouldn't listen and insisted on the girls drinking some hot tea with plenty of sugar in it before they left.

The vet's car was still at the farm and he was giving some last instructions to Major Parminter as the girls hurried up. A dejected and rather white-faced Jane was standing listening.

"I've given him a shot of cortisone," he was saying as he finished packing his instruments tidily into his bag. "And that should deal with the infection. He'll have to have the whole course which lasts five days—but you can leave that to me. Then there are the fomentations. They are most important. I've shown you exactly what to do, Jane, so that's your job. Make sure that the pad is hot enough and that you apply the bandage exactly as I did, otherwise he'll get it off at the first opportunity and it will be worse than useless. Put those on twice a day until I tell you to stop."

"And will he get well?" Cathy came forward and looked up anxiously into the vet's face. "Will he get really well again if we do exactly as you say?"

The vet was silent for a while, and then he said, "Look, young lady. I'm going to be absolutely honest with you, because it's no good my telling you anything that isn't true. Kelpie has a very tricky knee injury. There are three possible things that may happen. He may get completely well and be one hundred per cent sound again. We hope that is what will happen. Or the knee may heal quite well and the pony will be able to get around without much difficulty. His jumping days will be over, but nevertheless the knee will give him very little trouble, and you'll still be able to get quite a lot of fun out of him. Or—and this is looking on the black side of things remember—the pony may stay lame and never be much use for anything—except as a pet of course.

"I can't tell you at this stage any more than that, but I will remind you that good nursing and constant care over the next few weeks or months can make a power of difference to the way things will turn out. So, in a great measure, the pony's recovery is in your hands."

The vet pulled on his gloves and picked up his case.

"I'll come up again in the morning and give him his second injection, Major. Meanwhile keep him warm and quiet and give him small appetizing meals and plenty of lukewarm water to drink."

As the car drove away, Cathy and Belinda

followed Jane into the stable near the house, where Kelpie stood, looking very small and sorry for himself, in the farthest stall from the door. His right leg was tightly bandaged from shoulder to ankle, and every so often he fidgeted as if he was trying to find a comfortable position.

Cathy went quickly forward and slid her arms gently round the pony's neck. "Oh, Kelpie," she murmured, and her voice was thick with tears. The pony's ears moved forward and he turned his head and nuzzled her softly.

"It wasn't my fault," Jane said defensively in a small voice.

"Nobody said it was," Belinda said quietly.

"Oh, I know you think it was me," Jane said. "If I hadn't pushed him on when the others were getting ahead it would never have happened."

"No one has said it was your fault," Belinda said again.

"You don't need to say it," Jane said bitterly. "Saying isn't everything."

There was an awkward pause, then Jane spoke again, but this time her voice was so quiet and choky that the others could only just hear it.

"It was my fault actually," she said. "First we would have never gone on the paper chase at all today if it hadn't been for me. Belinda didn't really want to, I know, but I sort of forced her. And then it was my fault that Kelpie got kicked at the gate. I came up behind that grey far too quickly and suddenly Kelpie's nose was right on her tail. I should have given way, and taken my turn at the gate instead of trying to push my way to the front. It was me that deserved to be hurt—not Kelpie. That's why I feel so ashamed.''

It was the first time that either of the girls ever remembered Jane apologising for anything or admitting that she was in the wrong, and it took them so much by surprise that they just couldn't think of anything to say.

Jane took their silence for disapproval.

"I don't blame you for not wanting to talk to me,'' she said. "I shan't blame you if you never want to be friends with me again. I'm nasty and selfish and spoilt and horrid, and I don't deserve to have any decent friends, or a decent horse for that matter,'' and she knelt down in the straw by Kelpie's manger and burst into tears. Kelpie snorted, and, taking a careful step forward on his good leg, he bent his head and snuffled gently at Jane's hair. Jane put up a hand and gently stroked his nose.

"I think you forgive me, Kelpie,'' she whispered. "Horses are sometimes better than people that way.''

"There's nothing for us to forgive,'' Cathy said at last. "You didn't injure Kelpie purposely. It was something that could have happened to anybody. And as for the Bible Class—you were perfectly free to decide if you were going to come to that or not. I'm not in charge of you.''

"No, but God is,'' Jane said. "I was glad enough

to let Him be in charge when I wanted His help, but now that I can look after myself again, I sometimes forget all about Him."

"But everyone does, Jane," Cathy protested. "Even Joy, and she's one of the best Christians I know. I had a letter from her only this week, and she said it's very hard to remember about reading your Bible and praying to God, when the weather is so beastly hot that all you want to do is sink down in a chair and go to sleep. That's why I think God is so marvellous. He never gets huffy when we forget Him. He's just thrilled to bits when we remember He's our friend again!"

"Do you think He was punishing me when He let Kelpie have that accident? Because I went on the paper chase instead of going to Bible Class I mean."

"God's not like that," Cathy said firmly. "He doesn't dish out good marks if you go to Church or Bible Class, and punishments if you don't, as if we were in school."

"Then what's the good of going?" Belinda asked.

"I wish you wouldn't ask me all the questions!" Cathy said, running her fingers through her already untidy hair. "Going to Church is like going to visit someone you're fond of. Like Gran for instance. We go and see her because we love her, and want to let her know that we're thinking about her, and we're interested in what she's doing. We talk to her and she talks to us. That's what happens with God. And then again going to Church or

Bible Class is a way of learning more about God and the way He wants us to live, and it's a chance to meet other people who love God too. Like Pony Club is a way of meeting other people who love horses. You've got something in common with them, do you see? If we really love our relations we shouldn't just visit them when we've nothing better to do. Mummy says that is what's called 'making a convenience of them'. I'm not very good at explaining," Cathy confessed miserably. "I wish you'd ask someone else."

"Then you don't think God punishes us," Jane pressed, ignoring Cathy's last plea.

"No, I don't," Cathy said. "You know we've got the school exams coming at the end of term?"

The friends nodded, but looked puzzled, wondering what school exams had to do with Jane's question.

"Well, suppose you don't do any work at school and you skip through your homework, and then in the exams you come bottom of the class. Do you think that would be Miss Bright punishing you for not having worked better?"

"Of course it wouldn't," Belinda said, "It would be your own fault, and it would jolly well teach you a lesson."

"Then don't you see, when you get into trouble it's mostly your own fault as well. We go our own way without asking for God's help and advice and then things go wrong, and that's the way we learn. God doesn't *make* the wrong things happen, but when they do happen we often learn from them and take care that we don't let them happen again."

"I see what you mean," Jane said. "At least I think I do."

"It's going to be a full-time job looking after Kelpie," Belinda said, changing the subject. "He'll have to be fed and watered and groomed, and mucked out, as well as having these poultices changed twice a day. It will be a bit different to keeping him out."

"And he's going to get awfully fed up in here by himself," Cathy said. "Candy will wonder what on earth has happened to him."

"I can come up after school and help," Cathy said. "I can't do much in the morning because of the time, but I can help in the evening."

"Of course that will put paid to riding to school too," Jane said gloomily. "I'd forgotten about that."

"Well, the main thing is to try and get Kelpie better," Belinda said. 'Nothing else really matters, only that."

Chapter 5

HARD WORK

LOOKING after Kelpie proved to be a full-time job. The girls soon discovered that Kelpie at grass, and Kelpie in the stable, were two completely different things. Belinda and Jane had to allow a whole hour every morning to muck out the stable, put down clean straw, pick out Kelpie's feet and give him a rough grooming. Then his knee had to be poulticed and re-bandaged, and the pony had to be fed and watered.

It was still dark at half-past six each morning when Jane's alarm clock shattered the sweetness of their dreams, and the two girls lay in their warm beds, trying to summon up the necessary courage to throw back the blankets, and grope for their clothes.

"There's a lot to be said for a bicycle," Jane said wistfully one morning, as she was trying unsuccessfully to bandage Kelpie's knee, while the pony pawed the ground with his foot at the same time.

"Oh, stay still, will you, Kelpie!" she scolded the pony. "You might try and help, instead of hindering."

"It's coming undone from the other end," Belinda pointed out helpfully, and at that moment

55

the pony stepped back and ground the clean bandage into the straw.

"It looks so easy when the vet does it," Jane complained, starting all over again. "And Kelpie stands still for him."

"Perhaps it's us," Belinda suggested. "After all the vet has had slightly more experience than we have."

"Oh, Kelpie!" Jane said in disgust, as Kelpie, with complete disregard of his clean bedding, lifted his tail and gazed thoughtfully at his manger. Belinda went and fetched the shovel, and proceeded to repair the damage.

"I'll be glad when he's better," Jane said. "I'm just beginning to realize how fed up Father and Mother must have felt when I was ill. I never seemed to think of it at the time."

"The vet said it could take six months," Belinda pointed out. "Or even longer."

"I do hate not being able to ride," Jane confessed. "It's like having all the bother of a pony without any of the pleasure."

Belinda didn't say anything.

"I suppose you think I'm awful to feel like that," Jane said, feeling slightly ashamed.

"I suppose I was like that myself before last summer," Belinda confessed. "Although it was the other way round with me. I had all the fun of riding a pony with none of the fag of looking after it. Mummy and Daddy employed a man for the garden, you see, and he looked after Candy as well.

But somehow you don't get the same fun out of it," she went on reflectively. "I suppose it must be rather like having a Nanny to look after your children. You don't really get to know them—not like a real mother does."

"I only hope that stays on," Jane said, giving a final touch to the bandage on Kelpie's knee. Kelpie bent his head and inspected it.

"I know it's not as good as the vet's," Jane told him, "but it's the best I can do."

"I think Cathy has been pretty good over Kelpie," Belinda said. "She's come up every evening after school to help muck out and feed him, and it's not even her pony. She's got the long bicycle ride back afterwards as well."

"Cathy has got a special feeling for horses," Jane said. "Sometimes I think she loves them better than any of us. Really loves them I mean."

"We'd better go and get washed and changed," Belinda said, "or we'll be late for school. I'll borrow some of your talc too. We have Miss Turner for Geography this morning and she can't bear the smell of horses. 'Really, Belinda, you smell as if you've just come out of a stable;' she said to me last Wednesday. I thought she would think it was cheek if I told her I had!"

"Do you think Kelpie is getting any better, Daddy?" Jane asked her father, as they crowded three in the front seat of the jeep after breakfast.

"It's difficult to say," her father answered.

"Certainly the vet has coped with the infection. The wound looks clean enough."

"But he still limps," Jane pointed out.

"It's early days yet," Major Parminter said. "Once the wound itself has really healed he'll need a little gentle exercise. To stop the leg stiffening up."

"Riding?" Jane asked hopefully.

"No, leading," the Major replied.

Jane sighed. "Oh," she said.

"By the way, I see that Candy has broken out again," Jane's father went on. "She misses Kelpie I think. I must go and have a look at the field and try to find out where she's getting through. She needs some exercise too, young Belinda. She's getting fat."

"I know," Belinda said. "It was different when we rode them to school and back every day. It kept them fit. But now it's dark before we get home in the evening, and there's Kelpie to see to anyway."

"Cathy has been very loyal," the Major remarked, raising his hand to the driver of the milk lorry, who was coming up the hill. "She comes up every night to help you, doesn't she?"

"She likes doing it," Jane said.

"I know she does," her father agreed. "But it still means time and trouble."

"I've been thinking," Jane said suddenly. "I hope you won't just think this is because Kelpie is lame, because it isn't. I've been wanting to ask you about it for some time."

"Ask me about what?" the Major said.

"Well," Jane said, "Kelpie is getting a bit too small for me, that's all."

"And . . . ?" the Major questioned.

"And I wondered what you would say if I asked you to get me something a bit bigger."

"And what did you think I'd say?" her father wanted to know.

"I didn't know," Jane admitted. "But you see, I did have Kelpie when I was eight, and I'm now eleven. It makes a difference."

"Kelpie is very sturdy," her father pointed out. "I've ridden him myself on occasions."

"But he's not as big as Candy," Jane said.

"So you've got designs on Candy, have you?" the Major asked.

"Oh, NO!" Jane assured him. "I like Candy of course, but she's Belinda's pony, and in any case I've always wanted a grey. If I had a choice that is."

"And what do you suggest we do with Kelpie?" Major Parminter asked quietly. "It's not going to be easy to get rid of a lame pony, you know."

"I wasn't thinking of getting rid of him," Jane said hastily. "In any case I'd want to get him fit first. But you see, it may be weeks or months before I'm able to ride him again, and even then the vet can't guarantee he'll ever be a hundred per cent sound."

"I must say it suited me very well, you and Belinda riding to school and back," the Major said thoughtfully, as he drew up outside the school and lent forward and opened the door for the girls. "I'm not promising anything, mind, but I'll think about your idea. And if I do hear of a quiet pony, that I think might suit you—well, we could go and have a look at it anyway."

"Oh, thank you, Daddy," Jane said, giving her father an impulsive hug. "And you don't think I'm terribly, terribly callous over Kelpie, do you?"

"I think—I think you're Jane . . ." her father said wryly. "And I'm afraid I spoil you very much!" And with that he drove off.

Miss Bright was not only a pleasant person, she was also a good teacher, and she made her form work very hard. There was a hockey practice at morning break, and the three friends were on table duty at lunch time. Miss Bright asked for volunteers to prepare for the art lesson during the afternoon break, and so it was not until Jane's father had dropped them home at the farm after school that the matter of the new pony came up again.

"Do you think your father was serious about the pony?" Belinda wanted to know.

"What pony?" Cathy asked with interest.

"Jane asked her father about buying a new pony," Belinda told her. "She says that Kelpie is a bit small for her, and now that he's lame as well, she can't really ride at all."

"What will happen to Kelpie?" Cathy asked anxiously.

"I don't really know," Jane said slowly. "It

depends a lot on whether he gets fit or not, I suppose."

"Of course he's going to get fit," Cathy insisted. "He must, if we look after him properly."

"There's no must about it," Jane said with a shrug. "It's about an equal chance one way or the other, as far as I can see."

"But you can't sell him," Cathy pointed out. "You'd never be able to sell a lame pony."

"I don't think Daddy was thinking of selling him," Jane assured her. "Not at the moment anyway."

"Kelpie would hate it," Cathy said. "Seeing you ride another horse. It would make him feel awful. As if he was no good any more."

"You always think that ponies have minds that work like humans," Jane said irritably. "Horses aren't like that, I've told you before."

"Well, I think they are," Cathy said stubbornly. "Don't you Belinda?"

"Sometimes I think they are, and sometimes I don't," Belinda said tactfully, not wanting to be drawn into an argument.

"I thought I really had fixed that bandage properly this time," Jane said in exasperation a few minutes later, as they entered the stable to find Kelpie with yards of crepe bandage tangled round both his front feet. "You'd better put it on, Cathy. You seem to have got the hang of it."

"I get a book out of the library," Cathy confessed, "and practised on the legs of the dining-room chairs. It's easier on chairs than on a horse though. They don't keep walking round the room while you're practising, and they haven't got a knee half way down the chair leg either."

"If you do have another horse, how will you manage?" Cathy said, as she started to scrape the poultice on to the lint for a fresh dressing. "You'll never have time to see to Kelpie in the morning, and go and collect your ponies from the field, and get them ready to ride to school."

"Oh, we'll have to sort that out when it comes to it," Jane said. "Daddy hasn't actually agreed yet, you know."

"I'll just go and ask Mrs. Parminter if I can heat this up," Cathy said, balancing the poultice on her hand. "I won't be long."

"I hadn't thought about that," Belinda said, when Cathy had gone. "We can't get up much earlier in the morning or it won't be worth going to bed at all!"

"Perhaps Daddy will see to Kelpie," Jane said hopefully.

"You can't really expect him to do that," Belinda said. "He has an awful lot to do on the farm as it is."

"It's a pity Cathy doesn't live a bit nearer," Jane said. "There's nothing she'd like better than looking after Kelpie all by herself."

"I believe she would like it," Belinda said. "Even if she wasn't able to ride Kelpie at all. You know we are lucky, Jane," Belinda went on. "It must be rotten for Cathy. Loving horses as she does, and not being able to own one. It's hard to imagine how it must feel."

"It's also hard to imagine how one small pony can get in such a disgusting mess in a few short hours," Jane said, starting to remove the top layer of straw from Kelpie's stall with a pitchfork. "We'd better get a move on. I've got bags of homework tonight."

Cathy returned from the house with the poultice folded in a piece of rag. She applied it gently to Kelpie's leg, and bandaged it firmly into place. Then she washed round the pony's eyes, nose and dock, and filled his hay net from the loft. Finally the girls wheeled the barrow outside, and forked the manure on the heap in the yard.

Fred Bates, Major Parminter's man, was just starting up his motor cycle in the yard, and offered to give Cathy a lift home.

"I had a look at the pony today," he told her as he kept the engine revving outside Cathy's house. "He's looking a bit better, I thought."

"Did you really?" Cathy said, glowing with pleasure.

"Of course you can't tell really," Fred admitted. "Not while he's still in the stable and bandaged up like. But I fancy the leg was stronger than it was a week ago. Not so much local tenderness either. I reckon the vet will advise a bit of exercise when he's seen the old fellow next week. You just see if I'm not right."

When Jane and Belinda had gone to bed that

night, Major Parminter had a long talk with his wife about Jane's idea of a new pony.

"What do you think about it, my dear?" he asked Jane's new stepmother.

Mrs. Parminter put down the book she was reading, and sat staring into the fire for a few minutes without answering. "I don't really know what to say," she confessed at last.

"I feel it's good for Jane having to look after Kelpie. She's always been spoilt you know . . ." She silenced her husband's protest with a gentle movement of her hand.

"Oh, don't argue, John," she said. "Jane has been spoilt. It was only natural while she was ill, and I am to blame almost as much as you. It's good for her to have to discipline herself to get up early and look after Kelpie, especially without the reward of being able to ride him." She paused for a moment.

"On the other hand, I can see Jane's point. Kelpie is a little on the small side for her. It wouldn't matter just for hacking around, and having a bit of fun, but now that Belinda is living with us, and Jane's got the competition of Candy, well, I suppose it's natural that she wants a pony that can keep up. There's no getting away from the fact that it was very convenient when the girls were able to ride to school too. It takes quite a chunk out of your day to ferry them backwards and forwards."

"Any time that I should save on the taxi service would be cancelled out by looking after Kelpie," the Major pointed out. "With the best will in the world, I don't see how the girls could catch, groom and feed two ponies, and see to Kelpie before school as well,"

"Have you put it to them?" Mrs. Parminter asked. "They may have worked out a solution for themselves."

"The question of another pony only came up this morning," the Major said, "and I treated it very cautiously, and didn't hold out too much encouragement. I wanted to have time to think about it, and discuss it with you."

"Do you think Kelpie will get completely fit again?" Mrs. Parminter asked.

"It's difficult to say," the Major said. "Kelpie is very hardy, and these tough, half-breed ponies tend to mend quickly. On the other hand a knee injury is such a tricky thing. The vet seems to think the odds are slightly on our side."

"What will you do with Kelpie if he does get fit?" Mrs. Parminter enquired. "And what will you do with him if he doesn't, for that matter? If you do get another pony for Jane, you won't need to keep him, will you?"

The Major was silent for a while, and then he said. "There's young Cathy. We can't leave her out of it completely."

"But we've been through that before," Mrs. Parminter reminded him. "Cathy's parents cannot afford to let her keep a pony. Even if the pony was a gift in the first place."

"But she's devoted to Kelpie," the Major pointed out. "It would break her heart if we got rid of him. She's really much more attached to Kelpie than Jane is, come to that."

The Major stretched out his feet to the fire, and picked up a copy of the local paper that was lying on the side. For a while there was silence in the cosy sitting-room, but suddenly Jane's father lowered the paper, and spoke to his wife again.

"I didn't intend to do anything in a hurry about the ponies," he said. "But listen to this. . . . 'FOR SALE, GREY MARE 14.2. Suitable child's second pony. Quiet traffic. Good jumper. Owner outgrown. To good home.' "

"I think I must have a look at that," he said, "but I'll say nothing to Jane at present."

Chapter 6

"BELLE" AND JOY

THE next morning Major Parminter telephoned about the grey pony. Its owner lived in a small village a few miles out of Bedborough, and was quite willing for Jane's father to go over and see the pony that afternoon.

"What did you think of it?" his wife asked on his return.

"It's a nice-looking pony," the Major conceded. "There's no doubt about that. And it's in very good shape. Although of course I should get the vet to go over it first, if I did decide to buy."

"You don't sound altogether happy," Mrs. Parminter remarked. "Was there something about the pony that you didn't like?"

"There was nothing that I could put my finger on," the Major explained. "Mr. Lance—he's the owner—made no secret of the fact that the pony had plenty of spirit. That's why they advertised it as a 'second' pony. But that's not a fault in itself. Jane's a good rider, and she needs a pony that is not quite as easy as Kelpie. Something that would make her keep her wits about her, and be a kind of challenge."

"It's all right with traffic?" Mrs. Parminter said

anxiously. "That's one thing I would want to be quite certain about."

"Oh, yes, there's no difficulty there," the Major assured her. "It's certainly not a nervous pony, or anything like that. The child that's been riding Belle—that's the pony's name—is fourteen. Quite a bit older than Jane, and a good bit stronger too, I imagine."

"It wouldn't hurt to let Jane see the pony," Mrs. Parminter pointed out. "You'd find it easier to judge, once you'd seen her on its back."

"But if the mare appeals to Jane there'll be no stopping her. She won't let either of us have any peace until she's got her own way."

The Major was right! From the moment that Jane set eyes on Belle, she couldn't wait until the pony was her own. Belinda and Cathy watched with admiration, as Jane walked, trotted and cantered the pony round the paddock, showing off her paces.

"I'd like to see her jump," Major Parminter said to Mr. Lance, as the two men leaned over the gate watching the girl on the pony.

"I'll put up a couple of poles," Mr. Lance said quickly. "Perhaps you'd like to give me a hand." They carried four small oil drums into the field, and Belinda and Cathy helpfully placed some poles across them, making two jumps about two or three feet from the ground. Jane turned the pony's head towards them and kicked her into a canter. For a moment Belle hesitated, and laid her ears back, and then with a burst of speed she made straight for the jumps and sailed easily over them, with inches to spare.

"She jumps beautifully, Daddy," Jane said, glowing with excitement as she trotted the pony up to her father. "And she's got the most lovely paces. Please say that I can have her, please, please, please."

"How much are you asking?" the Major said quietly to the owner.

Mr. Lance hesitated. "I think she's worth a hundred and twenty," he said, after a short pause. "That's with the tack thrown in. But as your little girl has taken such a fancy to the mare, I'd accept a hundred. We particularly want her to go to a good home."

"I'd like my vet to go over her first," the Major said.

"Of course, there'll be no difficulty there," Mr. Lance agreed, "although I can assure you that Belle is quite sound in wind and limb."

Jane had slid to the ground, and was standing with the grey's reins looped through her fingers, listening eagerly to the conversation, and dancing with impatience.

"I tell you what," Mr. Lance suggested. "You get your vet to have a look at her tomorrow, and if everything is O.K., and you're quite satisfied, I'll bring her over in the box tomorrow night."

"Well, that's very kind of you," the Major said.

"But Jane could come over and fetch her. It's not very far."

"That's quite all right," Mr. Lance said quickly. "It won't take me more than half an hour to bring her over, and the evenings get dark so quickly now, you wouldn't want your girl to be out on her own."

And that was how the matter was left.

"Oh, Daddy, thank you!" Jane said gratefully, hugging her father's arm in the jeep on the way back. "She's absolutely super! I can't wait to ride her."

"Well, you'll have to," her father said dryly. "At least until Saturday. Tomorrow is Friday, and she won't be coming over until the evening anyway."

"You're very quiet, Cathy," the Major said. "What did you think of the pony? Did you like her?"

"She's very pretty," Cathy said cautiously. "And she can jump beautifully."

"But you did *like* her?" the Major persisted. "You haven't exactly answered my question you know."

"Oh, Cathy doesn't like any pony except Kelpie," Jane said with a laugh. "She's a one-horse girl. You ought to know that by now."

"You won't be getting rid of Kelpie, will you, Major Parminter?" Cathy asked anxiously. "At least not yet. You wouldn't try to sell him until he's quite fit again?"

"No, I shan't sell him until he's fit," the Major promised. "You can be sure of that."

"You'll have Cathy hoping he won't get fit again," Jane said in a teasing voice.

"Oh, *no!*" Cathy said in horror. "I couldn't be as selfish as that! It would be terrible if Kelpie never had the joy of cantering, and galloping freely again. It would be as bad as you being in your wheel chair Jane. You must see that!"

"I was only teasing," Jane said. "Don't take everything so jolly seriously."

"When people feel things deeply, it's hard for them not to take them seriously, Jane." Major Parminter said in gentle reproof. "You want to remember that."

"If we do decide to have Belle, what are we going to do about Kelpie?" the Major asked. "How will you manage to look after three ponies, and cope with the small and unimportant matter of school as well?"

"We can't get up any earlier," Jane said. "We get up in the middle of the night now!"

"Can't we keep the ponies in?" she went on. "That would save time catching them, and they wouldn't get so dirty either."

"I don't want to start keeping them in all the time," the Major said. "I've only kept Kelpie in the stable because of his leg. They've got perfectly adequate shelter in the field, and providing they get plenty of hay they're quite sturdy enough to stay out, you know."

"I've been thinking," Cathy said quietly. "I do hope you won't think it's dreadful cheek my butting in, and I haven't asked Mummy and Daddy about it yet. But if I got up early, really early I mean, I could come up and see to Kelpie before school."

"But it's miles and miles," Jane said. "Do be sensible."

"I am being sensible," Cathy said. "It's not all that far. About two miles from your house to ours, and I could bring my bike. That would make it much quicker."

"But it's dark in the mornings," the Major said. "Your parents would never agree to your coming all this way on your own, and I don't blame them."

"But I'd love to do it," Cathy said earnestly. "Really I would."

The Major hummed a little tune thoughtfully to himself for a while, as they speeded along the quiet roads. They were nearly back at the farm before he spoke again.

"There might be one possible solution," he said at last. "That is if your parents agreed. You usually come up in the evenings anyway, to help with Kelpie. Supposing I was to arrange for you to go back regularly with Fred Bates, on the back of his motor bike."

"What about Cathy's bicycle?" Belinda said. "She usually rides it up in the evenings you see."

"I've thought of that," the Major said. "She could leave her bike here in the evenings, and then perhaps I could arrange for Fred to pick her up in the morning. He starts work at seven anyway, you see. If you were really prepared to come up each morning, and see to Kelpie, he could bring you. And afterwards you could have a wash and change into your school things, and then go to school on your bicycle."

"That would be marvellous!" Cathy said "Oh, if only Mummy and Daddy will agree."

"Would you like me to talk to them?" the Major said. "Or Mrs. Parminter perhaps. We will if you like."

"Oh, would you!" Cathy said. "Grown-ups usually say 'yes' if they discuss it together because somehow it's not so easy to say no!"

"But would that be fair?" Jane said with a frown. "I don't see that Cathy is going to get much out of it."

"Perhaps Cathy doesn't want to get anything out of it," the Major said wisely. "There are some people who gain much more happiness from giving than getting, you know."

Jane had the grace to blush at the reproof, and was silent for the rest of the journey, her mind busy with thoughts of Belle and the fun she would have with the new pony. Cathy was thinking about Kelpie and wondering if she might ask God to help (just a little) in persuading her parents that looking after Kelpie would be a good thing. Belinda was thinking about her parents, and wishing, just a little bit, that she could find her mother waiting with open arms when they drew up at the lighted farm-house.

There was another letter from Joy waiting when Cathy got home, and Cathy opened it eagerly, before she even started her supper. Both Cathy and her parents had been anxiously awaiting news of Joy because Kuampuala had featured in the news-papers during the last week, and they wanted to know if Joy was all right. The word "coup" was a new one to Cathy, and she had had to ask her father what it meant when she had seen it staring up at her from the headlines of the newspaper.

"A coup usually means a sudden change of government," Mr. Smith explained. "Not a change of government because of an election, and voting, as we have in this country, but when a party of rebels arises, and overthrows the government, be-cause for some reason they do not think it is ruling in the right way."

"But that won't affect Joy, will it?" Cathy asked with a frown. "I mean it won't matter to teachers which government is in power. They'll go on teaching the children just the same."

"Well, it's not quite as easy as that," her father pointed out. "Sometimes, when there is a coup, the new government decide to alter completely the way things have been run. And this means that foreign people who have been working for the previous government, or with their approval, have to leave the country."

"But why?" Cathy demanded.

"I suppose the leaders of the new government want to put their own people in the key positions as far as possible," Mr. Smith said.

"Is Joy all right?" Mrs. Smith said anxiously, as Cathy opened the single sheet of airmail paper and started to read.

"I think so," Cathy said. "She says there has been a lot of fighting. And oh! Mummy—her uncle has been killed—oh, poor Joy!"

Mr. Smith quickly took the letter that Cathy held out to him, while Cathy gazed at him with a white face.

"It was an accident," her father said at last. "They were firing at random, during a street battle, and Joy's uncle just happened to get in the way. They've closed the school as well. I'm not surprised about that. It's amazing that Joy managed to get a letter out of the country. I should think the postal system is completely disorganized."

"Is there anything we can do?" Mrs. Smith wanted to know. "Joy hasn't got any parents, remember. It makes me feel responsible."

"I think she should come home," Mr. Smith said firmly, "but it's not the kind of thing you can arrange in five minutes at a distance of thousands of miles."

"What about the British Consul?" Mrs. Smith said. "I thought they were always there to help in an emergency."

"They probably have a queue a mile long," Mr. Smith pointed out.

"But Daddy, we've got to do something," Cathy said. "Joy may be in danger remember, and she'll be terribly, terribly lonely out there, all on her own."

"There's the Mission," Mrs. Smith remembered. "I am sure they would do anything they could."

"I don't really know what we should do," Mr. Smith confessed, running his fingers through his hair in a worried way. "There's always such confusion when something like this happens, and getting news of a particular person is almost impossible."

"But we know Joy is safe," Cathy reminded him, "because we've got her letter."

Mr. Smith picked up the letter again.

"This was written a week ago," he said. "The coup took place about ten days ago. The weekend before last I believe. Joy wrote this letter two days later. What has happened in the meantime is anybody's guess."

"Do you think it's any good getting in touch with the Missionary Society," Mrs. Smith suggested, "the one that Joy mentioned she had visited in Kuampuala? They must have a headquarters in this country. They would surely have news of their own people, and they might know something about Joy. It would be worth trying anyway."

"I'll phone them first thing in the morning," Mr. Smith promised. "But at present I don't see there is anything else we can do."

"Except pray," Mrs. Smith said quietly.

"Except pray," Mr. Smith agreed, and Cathy didn't need the written notice in her notebook to remind her to do that.

Chapter 7

A WONDERFUL SURPRISE

CATHY had decided that grown-ups were funny! She had quite expected her parents to say 'no' to her own and Major Parminter's plan for looking after Kelpie, but instead they had agreed! Cathy didn't know what the Major had said to persuade them, and she didn't really care. The one wonderfully important result of the interview, was that she was to be allowed to go up to the farm each morning to look after her beloved Kelpie, all on her own.

If it hadn't been for the thought of Joy, nagging at the back of her mind, Cathy would have been completely happy. Her father had phoned the Missionary Society in London as he had promised, but they had no news of Joy and very little of their own missionaries, apart from the fact that everyone was standing firm until the trouble had settled down a little. Cathy prayed every day for Joy's safety, and asked that God would show her and her parents any way in which they could be useful to Joy, or help her.

"It's awful not being able to do anything," Cathy complained to her mother one evening when she had returned from the farm. She had eaten her tea, and was trying to make up her mind to tackle her homework. "I keep asking God to show me if there is any way that I can help, but I don't seem to get any answer at all."

"Sometimes when we don't seem to get an answer to our prayers, it just means 'wait,' " Mrs. Smith reminded Cathy. "Perhaps there will be something you *can* do, if you only wait patiently, and keep on remembering Joy in your prayers."

"I never understand why it's so much easier to remember to pray to God when something is wrong, or you're worried about something, than when everything is going all right," Cathy remarked. "I haven't forgotten to pray once since we heard about the revolution. Have you?"

"We often find that we turn to God in trouble more quickly than we do at any other time," Mrs. Smith agreed.

"I do hope we shall soon have a letter or something," Cathy said. "Do you think it's wrong to feel happy about looking after Kelpie when Joy may be in dreadful danger?"

Her mother laughed. "It wouldn't be right to sit down and worry about Joy all the time," she pointed out. "Joy would hate you to do that, and it would be a way of showing that you don't trust our Heavenly Father to do the best thing possible for Joy anyhow. I am sure it's not wrong for you to enjoy looking after Kelpie. You're not finding it too much for you, are you?"

"Oh, no!" Cathy denied. "I just love it. And do you know, the vet said I can exercise Kelpie from now on. Not riding him of course, but walking him along the lane that leads to the pine wood and back, to get his muscles working again."

"The Major came to see Daddy and me today," Mrs. Smith said. "Daddy is on late turn at work as you know, and you were at school. He wanted to talk to us about something."

"What was that, Mummy?" Cathy said, bursting with curiosity.

"We told him to tell you about it himself," Mrs. Smith said with a smile.

"He's not going to get rid of Kelpie?" Cathy asked in sudden fear.

"No, he's not going to get rid of Kelpie," Mrs. Smith assured her. "Not really."

"I wish you'd tell me what he said," Cathy begged. "I shall never be able to settle down to equilateral triangles if you don't!"

"Of course if looking after Kelpie is going to interfere with your school work. . . ." Mrs. Smith said mischievously.

"Oh, Mummy, that's not fair," Cathy said.

"The Major said he'd see you tomorrow morning when you go up to the farm before school," her mother said firmly. "Until then you must be patient."

Cathy was just stuffing the hay into Kelpie's net the following morning when the Major came quietly into the stable, and stood by the door watching her.

"Kelpie is looking very fit," he said at last. "You're doing a good job."

"Well, of course he doesn't get himself all muddied up in the field at the moment, like the others." Cathy said fairly. "Jane and Belinda have an awful job to get Candy and Belle clean."

"I went to see your parents yesterday," the Major said.

"Mummy told me," Cathy said. "But she wouldn't tell me what you said."

"I asked her not to," the Major explained. "I wanted to tell you about it myself."

"It's not bad news?" Cathy said fearfully. "About Kelpie?"

"Nothing like that," the Major assured her. "Kelpie seems to be making very good progress. The vet is pleased with him."

"I've been very impressed with the way that you've looked after Kelpie," Jane's father went on. "I know you've always been fond of the pony, but it shows a really deep love of horses when you're prepared to spend time and trouble looking after them, with no thought of any reward."

"It hasn't been any trouble," Cathy said simply. "I love doing it."

"I know you do," the Major said. "That is why I have made up my mind to a certain course, and I'm glad to say your parents have agreed."

Cathy couldn't think what the Major was getting at. She did wish grown-ups would come straight to the point, instead of taking such a long time to say what they were going to do.

"It's not certain that Kelpie will completely

regain his paces again," the Major said, "although the vet thinks there is a very good chance. In any case he feels pretty sure that he will be fit enough for gentle riding, by someone who is not too heavy for him, and doesn't expect too much. I have therefore decided that I won't get rid of Kelpie, even though Jane doesn't need him any longer now that she has got Belle. I have decided to give him to you, Cathy."

For a moment Cathy's eyes shone with excitement and hope, then she sighed, and traced a pattern in the straw with the toe of her wellington.

"It's very kind of you," she said politely, "but Mummy and Daddy can't afford to let me keep a pony. Even if the pony was a gift."

"I know all about that," the Major said with a smile. "I haven't forgotten the last time I tried to give Kelpie to you, and you were disappointed. But this time it's going to be all right.

"You are to keep Kelpie at the farm, and ride him whenever you like, but the pony is to be yours. I am asking my solicitor to make out a proper deed of transfer to you, so that you will feel he really belongs. Last time I offered Kelpie, I felt he would have to be removed from the farm, because the constant sight of the pony would have upset Jane. Now everything is different. I wouldn't want to get rid of Kelpie anyway, so you see you're offering me an easy way out. You will take the responsibility and care of the pony off my hands, and yet I shall still feel we haven't cast him off at a time when he needs us most."

"And he's really to be mine," Cathy said, turning to the little bay, who had been listening with bright eyes and pricked ears as if he understood the whole of the conversation. "Oh, I just can't believe it," and she burst into tears!

"Well, that's a fine thing," the Major complained, taking out a large handkerchief and pushing it into Cathy's hand. "I thought you wanted a pony more than anything. And when I give you one, you burst into tears!"

"I just can't believe it's true," Cathy said, in a muffled voice, trying to talk and blow her nose at the same time. "It's like a fairy story."

"The important thing is that you realize the pony is really yours," the Major said. "If you ever want to sell him to buy another one, you're perfectly free to do so. Although of course I can't promise that the same conditions would apply to feeding and stabling another pony. We should have to talk about that. Jane will cease to have any claim on Kelpie, from now on, he will belong to you."

"Does Jane know? And is she pleased?" Cathy asked, a little doubtfully.

"Of course I know," Jane said, poking her head over the adjoining loosebox, and making Kelpie throw up his head with pretended fright. "I've been busting to tell you ever since Daddy first thought of the idea, but he made me swear a solemn oath that I wouldn't breathe a word. Belinda and I think it's an absolutely smashing idea, and I'm sure Kelpie would agree if he could only talk."

Kelpie tossed his head vigorously up and down, making his mane bounce.

"Look at him agreeing," Jane laughed. "Almost as if he understood."

"I'll never, never be able to settle down at school after this," Cathy said with a sigh. "Imagine trying to remember the names of Henry the Eighth's wives, when I've got this on my mind."

"You've got to be very, very careful that your school work doesn't suffer as a result of having Kelpie," the Major warned. "You don't want to give your parents any cause to regret their decision."

"Oh, I won't!" Cathy assured him.

"And there's one more thing to remember," the Major said. "There's no guarantee, as yet, that Kelpie will be a perfectly fit pony. He's still got a long way to go before the vet will pass him out, you know."

"If love can cure him, he'll get better all right," Jane said dryly. "We reckon Cathy mixes two parts of love with every part of the vet's poultice, before she puts the bandage on."

Kelpie softly nuzzled Cathy's face and hands, blowing down his nose very gently, his eyes warm with affection. Cathy slid her arms up around his neck and hugged him tightly, and then fastened the hay net to the manger, and gave him a last pat.

"I've told my solicitor to post the deed of gift

direct to you," the Major said to Cathy as they turned to go out of the stable. "I thought it would be more businesslike that way, and make you feel he was really yours . . ."

"Come on Jane," Belinda called from outside. "My hands are frozen holding Candy, and Belle keeps rubbing her nose down my raincoat and leaving a filthy mess."

"I'll go on," Cathy said, mounting her bicycle. "See you at school."

Cathy parked her bike in the bicycle sheds and unstrapped her satchel from her carrier. She still felt absolutely dazed with happiness, and she couldn't think of anything else but the wonderful and amazing fact that Kelpie now belonged to her. It was not until she was opening her satchel, and putting her books away in her desk, that she realized to her horror that she had still got her hat and coat on, and everyone was looking at her and giggling.

"I think you've forgotten something, Cathy," Miss Bright said calmly. "Be quick and nip along to the cloakroom before the bell goes."

"I'm sorry, Miss Bright," Cathy apologized. "I was thinking of something else."

The girls were filing past the teachers' desk at break when Miss Bright looked and caught Cathy's eye.

"And what were you thinking of this morning when you forgot to take off your coat and hat?" she asked with a smile. Cathy moved out of the line, and came to stand beside the teacher, her eyes shining with excitement.

"The most wonderful thing has happened to me, Miss Bright," she said. "I can't really believe it's true. It seems just like a beautiful dream."

"Indeed," Miss Bright said. "And may I hear what this wonderful thing is?"

"It's Kelpie," Cathy said. "The pony that used to belong to Jane before he hurt his leg, and before Jane had Belle. Major Parminter has given him to me for my very own."

"That's the pony that was injured in the paper chase, isn't it?" Miss Bright asked, showing a knowledge of her pupil's affairs that was very surprising.

"Yes," Cathy said. "But he's getting better now. I'm sure he is. And Major Parminter says I am to have him for my very own. I'm to keep him at the farm you see, so it won't cost Mummy and Daddy a penny. And I can ride whenever I like."

"That is certainly very exciting news," Miss Bright agreed. "I can see now how a small matter like removing a coat and hat slipped your mind completely!"

"Major Parminter says I am to have a deed of gift. I think that's some kind of paper. To show that Kelpie is really mine. The Major says I can do anything I like with him—even sell him— although of course I would never, never, never do that."

"Are you able to ride the pony again now?" Miss Bright wanted to know.

"Not yet," Cathy said. "But the vet says he is to be exercised. And that must show he is getting better, mustn't it? He doesn't limp at all now, only puts his foot down carefully, as if he's remembering that it used to hurt."

"It certainly sounds as if he is improving," Miss Bright agreed. "You must show me this wonderful pony one week-end. I would like to meet him."

"Would you really?" Cathy was delighted. "I should love to show him to you."

"And how is your missionary friend?" Miss Bright asked suddenly. "Joy, I think you said she was called."

"We're very worried about her," Cathy confessed. "There has been a revolution in the place where she was working. I expect you've read about it in the papers."

"I read about the African revolution," Miss Bright agreed. "But I didn't realize that your friend was working in the same district. Have you heard from her since the trouble started?"

"We had one letter," Cathy told her. "But that was several weeks ago. We do hope that everything is all right."

"I hope so too," Miss Bright said quietly. "But I expect that 'no news is good news', you know."

"Mummy says we must go on praying for Joy," Cathy told her teacher. "There doesn't seem to be anything else to do. Joy's uncle was killed in the fighting. That's why I worry about her. I can't bear to think of her being such a long way away, and all on her own."

"I expect you'll have a letter quite soon," Miss Bright comforted, "and I'm sure that you'll find you have no need to worry after all. And I'm delighted to hear about the pony," she finished. "And I hope that it won't be very long before he'll be perfectly fit again."

When Cathy joined Belinda and Jane in the playground she found Jane ruefully examining a nasty graze at the side of her right leg. The skin was broken in several places, and there was purple bruising around the outside of the wound.

"Whatever have you done?" Cathy asked in concern.

"Whatever has Belle done, you mean," Jane said bitterly. "I was opening the gate of Mr. Styles' yard this morning, and the little brute squashed my leg against the post before I could push the gate back. She tries it every time I open a gate, but this is the first time she's been too quick for me."

"Perhaps she's not used to gates," Belinda defended the absent pony.

"Then she'll have to get used to them," Jane said shortly. "I shall make a point of taking her through every gate on Daddy's land this week-end, and we'll soon see who is going to be master."

"It's funny about Belle," Cathy said slowly. "We all call her 'Belle' and it suits her, because she really is beautiful, but her name isn't spelt like that on her brow band. It's spelt 'Bel'—B-E-L—not B-E-L-L-E."

"I expect the letters have rubbed off," Jane said. "They do sometimes."

"Perhaps you're right," Cathy said, but she didn't sound really convinced.

Chapter 8

THE PROBLEM OF MONEY

IT was the first Saturday in December. The
ground was too slippery for riding, so the girls
had spent the afternoon cleaning their tack.

"Well, that's that!" Jane said at last, giving a
final polish to her stirrup iron and wiping her hands
on a piece of rag.

"We really shall have to get Daddy to add a bit
on to this shed," she went on, gazing critically
round the little cabin. "It's only just big enough
for one pony, let alone three."

"We could help him in the holidays," Cathy
suggested.

"But I shan't be here," Belinda said, pulling a
face. Belinda was going out to join her parents for
three weeks in the Christmas holidays, and Cathy
and Jane knew she was very excited about it,
although she tried not to show it.

"You know you're glad really," Jane said with
her usual frankness.

"I can hardly wait to see Mummy and Daddy,"
Belinda agreed. "It's not that I haven't been happy
here," she assured Jane quickly. "But I have
missed them. Much more than I thought I would.
You will take care of Candy won't you, and give
her lots of apples and carrots and things, so that

90

she doesn't feel lonely and left out while I'm away?"

"Of course we will," Cathy said quickly. "We'll exercise her too, so that she doesn't get too fat. It'll seem funny without you. I've got so used to its being the three of us."

"Well, I shall be back in January," Belinda reminded her. "It won't be all that long."

"Doesn't Kelpie look marvellous?" she went on as the girls leaned on the field gate watching the three ponies graze. "It doesn't seem as if there has ever been anything the matter with him apart from the scar on his knee, where the hair hasn't grown again yet."

"Daddy says it's thanks to Cathy that he has got well so quickly," Jane said. "The vet said that the regular poulticing and exercising helped enormously."

"Your father is generous," Cathy said softly. "I still can't really believe that Kelpie is mine."

"Well, Kelpie knows it's true anyway," Jane remarked, as the pony, hearing Cathy's voice, came trotting across the field, nickering gently all the way.

"The others are coming as well," Belinda said with satisfaction. "Do you remember how awful it used to be trying to catch Belle? At least she comes when she sees us now."

"Yes," Jane said. "But she's always so jolly independent. As if she doesn't really care if I'm there or not, but she's just coming to please herself."

Belinda laughed. "You're a bit like that too, Jane," she said.

"Like what?" Jane asked in surprise.

"Independent," Belinda said. "You often act as if you don't really care if people are friends with you or not. They can please themselves."

"I don't!" Jane said indignantly.

"Yes you do. Doesn't she Cathy?"

Cathy hesitated, and then truthfulness made her agree with Belinda. "You do rather, Jane," she said. "Although I don't really think you mean it."

"You'll be telling me I'm pig-headed next," Jane said a little touchily, "and go sideways or backwards when my rider wants me to go straight ahead! That's like Belle too!"

Cathy and Belinda didn't say anything.

"Well, say something!" Jane said. "Am I pig-headed or not?"

Cathy giggled. "Well, if you put it like that," she said.

"You have got a cheek," Jane said, turning away to scratch Belle's forehead over the gate. Belle stood for a moment peacefully, with her eyes half closed, enjoying the feel of Jane's fingers, then she suddenly made a sideways movement of her head and showed her teeth. Jane withdrew her hand to a safe distance.

"They'll be saying I bite next," she said shortly, half to herself.

"You do snap sometimes," Cathy remarked. "When people don't do as you say."

"I must be perfectly hateful," Jane said a little chokily. "I wonder you want to be friends with me at all."

"Don't be stupid," Cathy said. "It's only that it's just occurred to me that you and Belle are very much alike. You both like to get your own way. Neither of you likes to be told what to do. And both Belle and you sometimes are pig-headed and snap at people when they least expect it. The rest of the time Belle can be a perfect angel. She's nice to look at, has the most heavenly paces, and isn't afraid of anything in the world. She's not a shirker either. Ask her to do something and she'll put everything she's got into it."

"Thanks," Jane said. "I'm glad I've got something good about me anyway."

"I wonder if that's why your father bought Belle for you," Cathy said suddenly. "I wonder if he realized that you and Belle were very much alike, and he thought that you'd be good for each other."

"And I suppose you think you're like Kelpie?" Jane said a little wistfully. "Kind and affectionate and gentle and good-tempered, and always wanting to please."

"She is really," Belinda said after a moment's thought.

"I'm not!" Cathy denied hotly. "I might seem like that when I'm with you, because I'm always doing the things that I like doing best. But you should see me at home, when Mummy asks me to wash up when I want to come up and be with the horses, or if Daddy complains that my maths homework is disgusting, and makes me do it again. I'm not gentle and good-tempered then!"

"And what about Belinda?" Jane said. "How does she measure up to Candy?"

"Well, Candy is a thoroughbred," Cathy began.

"Do you want to see my pedigree?" Belinda asked with a giggle.

"And she can jump high," Cathy went on. "That's like Belinda being good at school."

"I'm not all that good," Belinda denied modestly.

"Oh, no!" Jane said. "And who came top of the form, and walked away with the General Progress prize?"

"See what I mean about the snapping?" Cathy said, keeping out of range.

"Candy is sensitive," Jane said thoughtfully. "It's very easy to hurt her feelings. Are you like that Belinda?"

"I am really," Belinda said, "although I try not to show it, because people think you're silly if you do. I feel things inside sometimes, but I find it hard to talk about them to anyone."

"What kind of things?" Jane said curiously.

Belinda had clambered over the gate and was stroking Candy with long soft stroking movements, as if she was stroking a cat. She went on stroking as she answered.

"I've felt inside me that I want to be a Christian. Like Cathy is," she said. "And I've asked the Lord

Jesus to be my Saviour and to help me. There—
I've told you now—and I suppose you think it's
silly just as I said."

"I don't think it's silly at all," Cathy said in
delight. "It's lovely to know. Joy will be glad
too. We've both been praying about you, you see,
and now God has answered our prayers."

"Have you really?" Belinda said in surprise.
"And I thought I'd done it all by myself."

"Well, you have, of course," Cathy said quickly.
"It's just that when people pray for you it's like
giving them an extra push."

"What about me?" Jane said. Jane could never
bear to be left out of anything for long. "Have you
been praying for me as well?"

"Yes, we have actually," Cathy said in some
embarrassment.

"Well, I think that's a bit of a cheek," Jane said
crossly. "Behind my back, and without me knowing anything about it."

"People aren't always very pleased if they know
you are praying for them," Cathy pointed out.
"They think that you're sort of criticising them,
and thinking that they're a bad sort of person. They
don't always like it."

"Well, your prayers might have been answered
for Belinda," Jane said in some satisfaction," but
they haven't been answered for me!"

"It's different for you," Cathy said quietly. "You
made up your mind to follow the Lord Jesus nearly
a year ago. When I hadn't known you very long.

It's just that you seem to have forgotten about it sometimes, and you let Him get rather a long way in front."

"I keep forgetting," Jane confessed. "I say and do things without thinking. And then I'm often sorry afterwards. But by that time it's too late."

"It's never too late," Cathy said. "You seem to think that once you've made up your mind to be a Christian you don't have to bother any more. It's like learning to ride a horse, and then thinking you know everything there is to know about them. You have to *learn* to live the Christian life, and believe me, it's a lot harder than learning to ride, I'm sure of that."

"Have you heard from Joy?" Belinda said suddenly.

"Yes, I meant to tell you," Cathy answered, fishing in the pocket of her jodhpurs for the thin blue airmail letter that had arrived that morning.

"Tell us what's in it," Jane said quickly. "I can never read grown-ups' writing quickly, so as to get the sense."

"Well, things are better in a way," Cathy said. "As far as the fighting that is. The shops and schools have opened again, and the rebels have formed a kind of government, although everyone still doesn't seem to be in agreement."

"Where is Joy living?" Jane asked.

"She's still living in her uncle's house." Cathy said. "But she won't be able to stay there for good. She doesn't know what will happen to the house, or

who her uncle has left it to. In any case, the
Government may requisition it. Daddy says that
means 'take it over for themselves'."

"Why doesn't she come home?" Jane said. "It
doesn't sound as if she's doing much good out
there. She could come and live with you and teach
at our school. That would be a jolly good idea."

"She says it would cost about a hundred pounds
for her to come home," Cathy said. "If the government decide to ban English teachers from the
schools, then she will have to leave the country.
She knows that. But she doesn't know where she
will get the money to pay the fare."

"Well, if they make her leave the country they'll
have to pay the fare," Jane decided. "That's only
right."

"They need you out there to manage things,"
Belinda giggled. "You'd soon have them all
sorted out."

"Supposing she was told to leave the country
and couldn't," Belinda went on. "Because she
hadn't got the fare, I mean. What would happen?"

"I don't know," Cathy said slowly. "If they
stopped paying her her wages for being a teacher,
I don't think she'd have anything. Of course the
people at the Mission might help her, but I don't
believe Joy would feel she could go to them, to get
her out of the mess. She went out on her own you
see, and not with any Missionary Society to back
her."

"A hundred pounds is a lot of money," Jane said

thoughtfully. "Now if it was ten pounds we might do something about it. I've got £1.35p in my money box. I was saving up for a new whip, but I'd rather give it to Joy if she needed it."

"How do you *get* money?" Cathy wanted to know. "I mean grown-ups always seem to have plenty of it. They must get it from somewhere."

"Well, you earn it of course," Jane said impatiently. "Like your father goes out to work."

"But your father doesn't go out to work," Cathy pointed out. "And he must get it from somewhere."

"Well. . . ." Jane racked her brains. "He gets it from selling things. Milk from the cows for instance. He always gets quite a big cheque every month for that."

"Is that all?" Cathy persisted.

"And he sells pigs," Jane went on. "And hay. And—oh, lots of things."

"I could sell my maths book," Belinda offered. "I'd be only too glad to see the back of it."

"That doesn't belong to you, silly," Jane said. "It belongs to the school. You can't sell things that belong to other people. They'd put you in prison if you did."

"Anyway, I don't think anyone would buy your maths book," Cathy argued. "It's got that enormous blot on the first page. The one you turned into a horse's head."

"What have we got that belongs to us and is worth a lot of money," Jane said thoughtfully. "That's what we've got to discover. And something we don't really want, either, so that we wouldn't mind getting rid of it."

"Isn't that a bit mean?" Belinda said. "It sounds as if we only want to help Joy providing it doesn't cost us anything. We ought to be prepared to sell something we really like. Then it would show that we really care."

"What about your new coat?" Jane suggested. "You like that, don't you?"

"Yes," Belinda admitted. "But I don't think Mummy would be very pleased if I sold it. She only bought it just before she went away. And I'm meant to wear it when I fly out to see them too. She'd have something to say if I turned up in my old raincoat. It's miles too short anyway. Mrs. Parminter says she's going to go shopping with me before we go back to school. So that we can buy a new one."

"Daddy gave me that super horse book for my birthday," Jane said. "He cut out the price inside, but it's jolly fat, and has got lots of pictures. I should think I'd get quite a lot of money if I sold that. I've read it anyway," She finished honestly.

"You don't get much for second-hand books however good they are," Cathy said wisely. "There's that funny shop at the end of the High Street that sells them, and there's hardly anything that's marked more than sixpence. And look at the Jumble Sale we held at the school. Some of the Annuals went for threepence, and they had cost about a pound when they were new."

"Well, that's that," Jane said, giving Belle a slap that made the pony leap into the air with all four feet at once.

"Don't do that, Jane!" Cathy said. "You know she hates it."

"I got so used to Kelpie," Jane confessed. "She wouldn't blink an eyelid if you let a bomb off under her front feet. It's hard to remember that Belle is always so jumpy."

As they walked back along the lane, Cathy was very quiet. She went to wait inside the barn where it was warmer until Fred was ready to leave on his motor bike. She was so deeply in thought that the man finally had to call her three times before he could catch her attention.

"Penny for your thoughts," Fred said cheerfully as he kicked the bike into action. "You looked as if you were miles away."

"I was," Cathy said. But she didn't explain to Fred exactly how far away her thoughts had been. In Kuampuala actually, with a friend who might have to leave the country very shortly because she had no job, but who had no money. A friend who might need a hundred pounds in a hurry, in order to enable her to pay for her fare home. A hundred pounds that, as far as Cathy could see, could only be raised in one particular way, and it was a way that Cathy just couldn't bear to think about.

Chapter 9

CATHY AND THE TEST

THERE were two letters for Cathy on the following Friday. Her mother had put them on the shelf so that Cathy could open them when she returned from her evening visit to the farm. One envelope was typed and looked very important, and at first Cathy couldn't really believe that it was meant for her.

"Someone must have made a mistake," she said to her mother as she frowned at the address.

"It's got your name on it," her mother pointed out. "I should open it."

There were two sheets of paper on the envelope. The first was a letter from Major Parminter's solicitor, and the second was a sheet of paper signed by the Major himself.

The paper read.

I hereby give to Miss Cathy Smith of 14 George Road, Bedborough, my pony KELPIE as a free gift and to be her absolute property.

Signed John Parminter,
Monks Coombe Farm,
Aggs Hill,
Bedborough.

Cathy gave a sigh of pure delight as her eyes

devoured the paper. Then she handed it to her mother.

"It's Kelpie," she said simply. "From the Major's solicitors. He said that he would."

"You really are a very lucky girl," Mrs. Smith said, coming round the table and giving Cathy a warm kiss. "But you will remember one thing, won't you? God must always come first in your life whatever happens. Never Kelpie first, and God afterwards. Or Daddy and I will feel that we have done the wrong thing in agreeing to Major Parminters' suggestion."

"Oh, yes, I will remember!" Cathy promised quickly, and then she stopped suddenly and amended her words slightly. "I'll try to remember anyway, Mummy, but it isn't always easy to do the right thing."

"It's seldom easy," her mother agreed. "But providing you're sensible over Kelpie and remember the lesson that Daddy once told you about the three-legged stool, and how Christians should be perfectly balanced people, then you won't go far wrong."

In the excitement of opening the solicitor's letter, Cathy had almost forgotten about the second letter which was an airmail one and from Joy.

Joy started her chatty letter with questions about Cathy and Kelpie, and her friends Jane and Belinda, and it wasn't until nearly the end that she mentioned the news that Cathy had been anxiously awaiting.

"I don't know if you will be glad or sorry to hear that I shall be coming home," Joy wrote. "I hope you will be glad to see me again, but I think you will be sorry that my time out here has been so short and has really been wasted. The new Government is very hostile to foreign teachers and we have all been given notice and instructed to leave the country at our earliest convenience. This was a great blow, although of course not entirely unexpected. My friends on the Mission Station are also packing up, which is very sad as they have been working in this part of Africa for nearly thirty years. I know now that I was wrong to come out here by myself, and perhaps I misunderstood God's plan for me when I refused to listen to the Society who gave me advice. I did not fully realize that they knew the situation out here far better than I could hope to do."

"She's coming home, Mummy," Cathy said, turning over the page to read the last paragraph of Joy's letter.

"I do not quite know what to do about money," Joy wrote. "My uncle's estate still hasn't been settled, and I cannot accept financial help from the Mission, although they have most kindly offered to advance my fare home. Somehow I do not feel that this is what God wants me to do. Every time I decide to go and see my friends, and tell them that I will accept their help, it is as if something is holding me back. Please continue to pray for me, Cathy, that I may be sure this time of what

God wants me to do, and be prepared to do it."

"I think she's silly not to let the Mission help her," Mrs. Smith said, when she had finished reading the letter that Cathy passed to her. "She could always pay them back after she had worked in this country for a little while. Sometimes I think one can be too independent."

"But she says she doesn't feel that this is what God wants her to do," Cathy pointed out, referring once more to Joy's letter which her mother had returned to her. "It's very hard to know when God is leading you," Cathy complained. "I do wish He'd put it down in black and white."

Her mother laughed. "Well, He has in a way," She said. "He's given us the Bible, hasn't He?"

"But that is about people who lived a long time ago," Cathy argued. "It's not about you and me and Joy and Kelpie, and things like that."

"No," her mother agreed. "But people don't change very much you know. It's usually possible to find someone in the Bible who had a similar problem to the one that we are trying to sort out, and when we read how God led them, it helps us to sort out our own problems in roughly the same way."

"But how do we find people like us in the Bible?" Cathy wanted to know. "It's a very long book."

"That's one of the reasons why it's useful to read your Bible every day," her mother said. "As you get older you'll gradually read your way right through it, and then when you have a problem, certain parts of it will come to your mind, and you'll turn them up and find they have a special meaning for you."

"What about Joy?" Cathy said. "I wonder what part of the Bible she turned to to make her feel that God didn't want her to leave Africa with the other missionaries."

"You do expect me to answer questions right out of the blue! Don't you, Cathy?" her mother laughed. "Well, let me think. . . . There's a story of the Moabites who wanted Balaam to go back with them to their own country," she said slowly. "Get me a Bible and let me see if there is any help in that."

Cathy fetched her mother's Bible from the top of the bookcase, and Mrs. Smith started to turn its pages.

"Here it is," she said at last. "The story is in Numbers Chapter 22. Balaam didn't feel it was right to go with the Moabite princes you see, so he told them, 'Go to your own land; for the Lord has refused to let me go with you'."

"But he did go in the end," Cathy pointed out. "That's the story of Balaam and his ass, isn't it? Didn't an angel appear and stand in the middle of the road and the donkey saw the angel, but Balaam didn't?"

"That's right," her mother said. "You see in the end it was God's will that Balaam went to Moab, but not in the beginning. I've only shown you this story just as an example of how we can

sometimes use the Bible to find out what God
wants us to do."

"Do you think Joy has been reading this story,
then?" Cathy wanted to know.

"She may not have," Mrs. Smith said, "she may
may have read something completely different. But
it has still made her feel that God is speaking to
her in a special way."

"But it could be accident," Cathy said. "You
could just turn to a story and it needn't be really
meant for you at all."

"That's why it's so important to pray as well,"
Mrs. Smith agreed. "Reading our Bibles, praying,
and listening to the Holy Spirit speaking to our
minds. That's the only way we can be sure."

Cathy went upstairs to get ready for bed shortly
afterwards, and she knelt by the bed and laid her
closed Bible on the bed in front of her.

"Please God, tell me what to do about Joy,"
she said, closing her eyes and laying her head upon
the counterpane. "Please tell me if this idea about
Kelpie is just something I've thought about for
myself. Or if it really is a message from You. And
please God, if it is a message from You, make me
brave. . . ." and then the tears welled out from
Cathy's tightly-closed eyes and she sobbed bitterly.
"It's no good, God," she said in a choking voice. "I
just can't get rid of Kelpie now. I can't, I can't, I
can't!"

After a while Cathy stopped crying, found a
hanky in her skirt pocket and blew her nose. Then

she went into the bathroom and washed her face in warm water, and rubbed some talcum powder on the red blotchy places, so as to help it not to show. She went back into her bedroom, and picked up her Bible again, and opened it at the portion for the day. Cathy wasn't all that keen on the Old Testament for she sometimes found it rather dull, but Mummy had said it was wrong just to read the easy bits because all of the Bible was useful, and so Cathy had persevered. Genesis 22. 1–10. Cathy glanced at the Chapter and saw that it was one that she knew very well. It was rather a sad story in a way, but it had a happy ending, even though the people in the story didn't know that in the beginning. She started to read.

"After these things God tested Abraham and said to him, 'Abraham' and he said 'Here I am'. He said, 'Take your son, your only son Isaac, whom you love and go to the land of Moriah, and offer him there as a burnt offering upon one of the mountains of which I shall tell you'."

Cathy stared at the words, remembering how she had talked to her father about them the very first time she had read the story some years ago.

"I think it was horrid of God to test Abraham like that," she had said to her father. "He must have known that Abraham loved Him, and He knew He wasn't going to make him kill his son in the end, so why did God have to get Abraham so upset?"

"I think Abraham was testing himself in a way,"

her father had replied slowly. "Perhaps his son Isaac had become so important to him that he couldn't think of anything else, and perhaps one day he thought to himself, 'I wonder if I had to choose between my son and God? Who would I choose?' Perhaps the story you have been reading was the result of his thinking."

Cathy looked at the story again. But in her mind she changed the words a bit, until they read.

"After these thing God tested Cathy and said to her, 'Cathy!' and she said, 'I'm here'. He said, 'Take your pony, your only pony Kelpie, and sell him so that you can show that you love Me and Joy by providing the money for her fare back to England.'"

"I can't!" Cathy said.

"You can!" a Voice inside her seemed to answer.

"No, I can't!" Cathy said, and she seemed to shout it in her mind even though no words came out.

"You won't, you mean," the Voice said sadly.

"But why?" Cathy argued again.

"To show you love Me," the Voice said silently. "And to show you love Joy."

"But he's mine," she pointed out.

"I gave my only Son to die for you," the silent Voice seemed to remind her.

"But you are God," Cathy complained.

"And you are a daughter of God. I have given you My strength," Cathy's inner Voice said finally, and then He didn't say anything else.

When Cathy's mother came to tuck her up she thought she was already asleep, for she was curled in a tight little ball with her face hidden under the bedclothes. She gently kissed the top of her head, and turned out the light, but it was many hours later before her daughter fell asleep finally, and even then thoughts of Kelpie and Joy followed her into her dreams.

Next morning she got up early, although it was Saturday, and purposefully tore a page out of the back of her school rough notebook. She took a pencil with a fairly sharp point out of her pencil box and started to write out a notice.

FOR SALE. BAY GELDING. VERY QUIET. SWEET TEMPERED. 13.2. £100. APPLY SMITH, 14 GEORGE ROAD.

She opened her money box and took out the five shillings that Aunt Mary had sent her for her birthday, and put it on top of the note. Then she went down to breakfast.

She managed to eat half a piece of toast and drink a cup of tea, explaining to her mother that she wasn't really hungry. Then she cleared away and washed up and went upstairs to make her bed.

"Perhaps no one will answer," Cathy comforted herself as she straightened the rather crumpled sheets, and shoved her pyjamas under the pillow in an untidy heap. "I can't help it if no one answers. I will have done what God wants me to, and perhaps everything will work out all right. It did for Abraham after all, I won't tell Jane or her father about the advertisement. They wouldn't understand anyway. And after all Major Parminter did say that Kelpie was mine and I've got a paper to prove it."

The advertisement appeared that night in the For Sale column of the *Bedborough Echo*. Miss Bright might not have seen it but for the fact that her brother needed a garden roller, and Miss Bright had thought she might buy him one for a surprise. She could hardly believe her eyes as the advertisement caught her eye.

"What an extraordinary thing," she said aloud as she read it once again.

"What's extraordinary?" her brother inquired as he folded up the playpen and tried to ease a heap of his small son's toys under the sideboard with the toe of his shoe.

"This advertisement," Miss Bright said. "There's a girl in my class called Cathy Smith. She's terribly keen on horses and when she came to school a few weeks ago she was absolutely radiant. Apparently a Major Parminter, father of another child in my class, had given her a pony. The pony was sick and Cathy had been nursing it. It's quite a long story but those are the main facts."

"Lucky Cathy," Bill Bright said dryly.

"But that's not the point," Miss Bright explained. "In the paper tonight there's an advertisement offering the pony for sale. I just couldn't believe my eyes."

"Perhaps the kid is having another one," Bill Bright suggested. "It does happen you know."

"Not to Cathy," Miss Bright said firmly. "Her parents have a job making both ends meet as it is. That's why having the pony given to her was such a wonderful thing."

"Do you think there's a story behind it?" Bill Bright came and sat on the arm of his sister's chair, and took the paper from her.

"I thought I'd arouse your professional interest," Miss Bright said, looking up with a smile. "Just drop a hint of 'human interest' in front of a newspaper reporter, and he's off like a streak of greased lightning!"

"But do you think there might be a story behind it?" her brother persisted, ruffling his sister's hair in a way that would have appalled the members of her class if they had been present.

"There's more in this than meets the eye," Miss Bright said firmly. "That I do know. And I shan't rest until I've found out the facts."

Chapter 10

HOW THINGS WORKED OUT

CATHY was rather glad that Belinda had left England for her visit to her parents in Hong Kong. At least it was one less person to know about Kelpie. She had decided that she would not tell anyone about the advertisement because, after all, perhaps no one would answer it, and then it would just prove to be a lot of fuss about nothing. If her mother and father, or Major Parminter, happened to see it, then she supposed she would have to explain, but otherwise it was to be something between herself and God.

"A man called in to see you today," her mother said when Cathy arrived home from school on the Monday. "I told him that I did not expect you home until about half past five. I thought that you would be going up to the farm first to see to Kelpie."

"I decided not to," Cathy said briefly. "He's much better now, and is out in the field with the others, so he gets his own exercise. Jane said she would give him his hay when she fed the others."

"The man didn't say what he wanted," Mrs. Smith said. "He just said he wanted to speak to you. You haven't been doing anything wrong have you?"

"Of course not," Cathy said, going quite red, the way that some people do if they're accused of doing something wrong, even though they haven't done it!

"He said he'd call back," Mrs. Smith went on.

Suddenly Cathy felt sick. Supposing the man had come in answer to her advertisement? Oh! surely God couldn't let her down like that. After all, He had saved Isaac for Abraham just as soon as He was sure that the old man really loved Him best, surely, surely, He wouldn't ask her to give up Kelpie completely?

"I think I'll get on with my homework," Cathy said, really wanting an excuse to sit down and think without anyone talking to her. "I've got rather a lot, so I'll do it upstairs."

"Don't forget to put on the electric fire," her mother reminded her. "It will be cold in your bedroom."

Cathy got out her geometry text book and opened her rough notebook to check the numbers of the set work, and that was as far as she got. She kept thinking about the man who had called and who was coming back, and Kelpie grazing so unsuspectingly in his field, and Jane who wouldn't understand and would be simply furious.

"If I thought that you would sell Kelpie I'd have never let Daddy give him to you!" She could almost hear Jane saying the words.

She wasn't even absolutely sure that her parents would agree. She knew that her mother had very strong views about getting rid of gifts that had been given to you. She wouldn't even let Cathy give away the very dull book called *Britain in the Middle Ages* that Aunt Amy had given her for a birthday present. Cathy had suggested passing it on to Wendy Fuller, who had only asked her to her party anyway because her really proper friends had all had measles, and couldn't come.

"Of course you can't give away something that has been given to you as a present!" her mother had said. "Whatever would Aunt Amy say if she knew!" And so *Britain in the Middle Ages* was still on the top shelf of the bookcase, and Cathy hadn't even bothered to cut some of the pages that were stuck together.

If her mother thought it was wrong to give away *Britain in the Middle Ages* which had only cost 75p—and probably less—because there had been a cheap sale offer ticket stuck over the price which Aunt Amy had forgotten to peel off— how would she feel about Cathy selling Kelpie, which in a way was even worse than giving him away?

Cathy hadn't done any homework at all in a whole hour. She had drawn pictures of Kelpie in her rough notebook, and written 75p in lots of fancy ways around the outside. Then she had added a border of question marks, varied with the words Jane and £100 until the whole page looked rather a mess.

Suddenly she heard a knock at the front door, and she leapt out of her seat.

"I'll go!" she shouted to her mother, taking the stairs two at a time, and sliding along the hall on the mat.

The man who stood at the door looked rather nice, although Cathy hated him at first sight!

"Good evening," he said politely. "I saw an advertisement in the paper about a pony. This is the right house, isn't it?"

"Yes," Cathy said. "I suppose so. That is. . . ." she went on. "Of course it is. Do you want to buy him?"

"That depends," the man said cautiously. "I should want to see him first, of course."

"He's a lovely pony," Cathy said. "I'm afraid you'll like him."

"Afraid?" the man said with a smile. "But I thought you wanted to sell him."

"Of course I don't," Cathy said crossly. "No one would. He's so gentle and intelligent and he's got the sweetest nature. Of course I don't want to sell him."

"But you put an advertisement in the paper," the man reminded her. "Offering him for sale." He pulled a copy of Saturday's *Echo* out of his pocket, and pointed to the place where he had marked Cathy's advertisement with blue biro.

"Oh, yes," Cathy said. "Of course I want to sell him. That's why I put the notice in the paper."

The man ran his fingers through his hair in some bewilderment. "I am afraid we're talking at cross purposes," he said. "Let's start again."

"I'm going to sell the pony, but I don't want to," Cathy explained quietly. "That's what I was trying to say."

"I see," the man said, although he didn't really see at all. "Would it be a very rude question to ask why you are going to get rid of him? He's quite sound, isn't he?"

"Oh, yes," Cathy said quickly. "Kelpie did hurt his knee a couple of months ago, but he's much better now. It's all right to ride him again, providing you don't go mad of course. And he'll get stronger every day."

"When can I see him?" the man asked.

"Well, I could take you up to the farm to-morrow," Cathy said slowly, "but it would have to be after school."

"I see you're asking £100 for Kelpie," the man said. "That seems rather a lot. Especially for a pony that's had a bang."

"Well, I can't take any less," Cathy said. "I'm not even sure that will be enough."

"Enough for what?" the man asked.

"Enough for Joy's fare," Cathy snapped.

"Who is Joy?" the man said.

Suddenly Cathy realized she had said more than she meant to.

"That's got nothing to do with selling the pony," she said firmly.

"I'm sorry," the man said. "I was just interested. I'll come and see Kelpie after school then. Where shall I meet you?"

"At the top of Agg's Hill," Cathy said, "just where the roads divide. I'll be there at half-past four."

"Right," the man said. "I'll see you then."

"Was that the man who called earlier?" Mrs. Smith asked, as Cathy trailed slowly into the kitchen after closing the front door.

"Yes," Cathy said. "It was only about an advertisement he had seen in the paper."

"I suppose he'd got the wrong house," her mother said. "He might have told me earlier. It would have saved his coming back."

Cathy didn't answer. It was a good way out of the situation and she hadn't had to tell a lie.

Mr. Bright was in high spirits when he reached home. His sister was turning some chips on the gas stove, and the smell suddenly made him feel very hungry.

"Who is 'Joy'?" he asked his sister, coming up behind her and putting his hands on her shoulders.

"I haven't the faintest idea," Miss Bright said. "I do wish you wouldn't produce questions out of the blue and expect me to know the answers!"

"But you must know!" her brother persisted. "I went to see the kid who is selling the pony this evening, and she let it slip that she's selling the pony to pay 'Joy's' fare. Who is Joy? That's what I want to know."

"Joy," Miss Bright said slowly, turning away from the stove. "Joy. That's the girl who has gone out to Kuampuala as a missionary teacher."

"Kuampuala," her brother said sharply. "The revolution?"

"Yes," his sister said. "Cathy was telling me about it the other day. I'm beginning to see now. Joy has to leave the country. She went out there on her own you see, without Society backing and is finding great difficulty in raising the fare. Cathy must be trying to help by selling Kelpie."

"The poor kid," Mr. Bright said. "But a hundred pounds will be nothing like enough. It must cost a hundred and fifty single at least. That's by air."

"I don't suppose that Cathy knows that" Miss Bright said. "A hundred pounds must seem a great deal of money to her."

"What a story!" Mr. Bright said with shining eyes. "SMALL GIRL SELLS HER PONY TO PAY MISSIONARY'S FARE BACK. Can't you see the headlines! The Editor will give me all the space I need. I'm sure of that. It will melt the readers' hearts and the money will pour in. My name won't be Bill Bright if it doesn't."

"To you it may be just a good story," Miss Bright said quietly. "But don't forget that to Cathy it's the biggest sacrifice that she's ever been asked to make, and no one can know what it cost her to put that advertisement in the paper."

"But she won't have to get rid of the pony! Don't you see that?" Miss Bright's brother pointed out. "She'll be able to keep Kelpie and still get her friend safely home. I'm going to start on the article now. Try and keep your nephews quiet, there's a dear."

"But what about the supper?" Miss Bright wailed, brandishing the pan of chips. "I made Kay go and lie down and I'm meant to be in charge of supper."

"It will keep," Bill said. "Stick it in the oven and I'll have it later."

It was ten o'clock before the reporter was satisfied and came to retrieve his soggy supper from the bottom of the oven.

"I'll see Cathy tomorrow as arranged," he told his sister as he was eating. "If I'm careful I can get a few more details from her without her suspecting. I'd like to get hold of a snap of the pony too. And of Cathy for that matter. There's nothing like a few pictures to make an appeal. I want to check up on the details of the Kuampuala rising too. Make sure I've got my facts straight. And ring the air-line to find out the exact fare, although I know it's a good deal more than the kid expects."

"Supposing someone else buys the pony first?" Miss Bright said quietly. "Have you thought of that?"

"Not a chance," her brother said. "No one would buy a pony without seeing it, and it's kept on Agg's Hill. Cathy couldn't take anyone up before tomorrow, and I'm meeting her right after school."

Bill Bright was as good as his word. He saw Kelpie at half-past four and by seven o'clock the following evening the article was ready for the press. He gave the typed copy to his sister to read. When she had finished she laid the sheets down on her lap and gave her brother a straight look.

"There's one thing missing," she said. "You haven't mentioned that Cathy's decision to sell the pony was made because she is a Christian, and she felt that this was what God would have her do."

"Oh, drat it, Sue," her brother said irritably, "you can't expect me to put that in an article. The public don't want me to preach at them."

"Sometimes it doesn't hurt the public to get a sermon," Miss Bright insisted quietly, "especially when the sermon shows faith in action, as Cathy's sacrifice shows it. You must please yourself of course. But you pride yourself on faithful reporting. And faithful reporting means telling the whole story, not just the angle you think will be the best news value."

"You win," her brother said after a short pause. "Although if the boss edits it, don't blame me."

"I won't," Miss Bright promised.

And so, the next day, *The Bedborough Echo* carried the story of Kelpie, and the girl who had been prepared to sell her most treasured possession because she was sure that this was the thing God wanted her to do.

And people who had not been to church for years, and had forgotten what praying was all about, read it, and were ashamed, and made up their minds that they would do better in future.

And old ladies read the story, and toddled down to the Post Office with their Pension Books and bought a 10p Postal Order, and slipped it in an envelope addressed to the *Echo*.

And business men read the article as they toasted their toes before a roaring fire, and waited for dinner, and pulled out their cheque books, and scribbled their name at the bottom of a cheque.

And children read it and counted the money in their piggy banks, and decided they could well spare sixpence to help bring the missionary lady home again.

And housewives read it, and altered the following day's menu from chops to cheese pie, and slipped their savings in an envelope, and popped it through the *Echo*'s letter box.

And Major Parminter saw it and said "Well, I'm blowed!" and handed it to Jane, who didn't say anything at all, for once, although she thought all the more.

And Mr. and Mrs. Smith read it, but they didn't show it to Cathy because they thought she would hear about it soon enough, and they didn't know about the money that was already pouring into the *Echo* Office. But their hearts were very full, and very thankful, and they were very, very proud of their daughter who was brave enough to do the right thing, however much it cost.

When Cathy arrived at school the following day

she found that she was a heroine, but at first she couldn't understand why! And when she did understand, she couldn't think how everyone knew. And then someone showed her a newspaper, and she realized that the gentleman who had come to look at Kelpie, and had gone away without buying him, had not been an ordinary buyer, but a newspaper reporter, and in fact he was the brother of their teacher Miss Bright.

Miss Bright called her out into the corridor just before prayers in order to have a few words in private.

"You've been very courageous, Cathy," she said. "I'm proud of you."

"But I didn't want anyone to know," Cathy said in distress. "Jane will be furious. She hasn't had time to say anything yet, because she was late coming down from the farm, but she will later, and I know she won't be pleased."

"But the pony was yours," Miss Bright pointed out. "You told me so."

"Oh yes, I know," Cathy said, "but that won't make any difference to Jane, you'll see. And I don't think Mummy and Daddy will be very pleased if they hear about it. They don't like me to give presents away, let alone sell them. I wanted to do it all in secret," she explained. "And now it's all gone wrong."

"I don't think you'll find it's 'gone wrong' at all," Miss Bright said gently. "My brother thinks that people will be really interested in Joy, and will

send in the money to pay her fare home. Even if
you had sold Kelpie, a hundred pounds wouldn't
have been enough money you know. My brother
says the fare is about one hundred and fifty pounds."

"Is it really?" Cathy said. "She's only coming
one way, you know."

"I know," Miss Bright said. "One hundred and
fifty pounds is the single fare. And there's another
thing," she went on. "The article my brother wrote
may really wake people up to the fact that there
are such people as missionaries. Just think how
wonderful it would be if the local churches really
decided to adopt Joy as their very own missionary,
and to provide for her and her work."

"But she's coming home," Cathy pointed out.

"But she won't stay home," Miss Bright said.
"Once she is sure of God's plan for her. I am sure
she will want to go out again. Not to Kuampuala,
of course, but there are many other places that
are desperately in need of trained teachers, who
can also teach people about God's love."

At the end of three days the *Echo* had to close
the "Kelpie Fund", as it was called, for over £500
had been donated to pay Joy's fare home from
Kuampuala. Mr. Bright arranged all the details,
and, just three days before Christmas he took Miss
Bright, Jane and Cathy and her parents up to
London in his car to meet Joy's plane. Jane had
insisted that she was one of the party.

"After all, Kelpie did used to belong to me,"
she pointed out. "And if it hadn't been for trying to

sell Kelpie all of this would never have happened."
And so Mr. Bright had agreed to let Jane join the
party, even though it would be rather a squash.

"I'm so happy I could burst!" Cathy said as they
sped along the deserted roads early in the morning.

"Well, don't burst here," Jane said sensibly.
"There's no room."

"Life is exciting," Cathy went on. "You never
know what will happen next."

"You don't on Belle," Jane agreed. "She threw
me into Dad's manure heap last night, just because
a mouse ran across the yard while I was tightening
up the girth. I smelt disgusting for the rest of the
evening even though I had a bath and smothered
myself with Mother's Ashes of Roses talcum
powder afterwards."

"Now that we've got Joy off our minds we can
concentrate on Belle," Cathy said slowly. "I meant
to show you something funny about her bridle, that
I discovered the other day. I think it will give us
a clue to understanding her."

"What was it?" Jane wanted to know. But
Cathy wouldn't tell her, even though she pestered
all the way to London!

They waited in the airport lounge until Joy's
plane was announced, and then they went to the
custom's hall and stood by the door. As a tall,
brown Joy came through the doorway, Cathy
broke away from the little party, and hurled herself
in Joy's arms.

"What a lovely welcome," Joy said chokily as

she hugged her friend warmly. "I didn't expect a reception committee to meet me."

Mr. Bright came forward to shake hands, but Joy was looking beyond him with a surprised expression, her face alight with pleasure.

"Sue!" she said. "I can't believe it."

"Joy!" Miss Bright hurried towards Joy while everyone stood and stared in amazement.

"Joy Wills! I never thought! But then Cathy never mentioned your surname, and Bill didn't put it in the article. Why did it never dawn on me, I wonder, that it might have been you?"

"We haven't written for ages," Joy confessed. "Not since we were at College, I'm ashamed to say. But it's wonderful to see you again."

"This is my brother," Miss Bright said, "And of course Cathy's parents you know."

"And me!" Jane said, bouncing up and down, and determined not to be left out of it.

"It's going to be a squash," Bill Bright warned. "I hope you don't mind."

"Mind?" Joy said. "I don't think I shall ever mind anything again, now that I am back home among my friends."

It was the happiest Christmas that Cathy could ever remember. On Boxing Day there was a party at Monke's Coombe with Miss Bright and her brother and sister-in-law and the boys, and Cathy and Mr. and Mrs. Smith and Joy.

"It's sad that Belinda isn't here," Jane said. "She's really missed all the fun."

"It wasn't all fun," Cathy said. "Not when I thought I'd have to sell Kelpie."

"But you didn't," Jane said briskly. "And that's all that matters. You've got Kelpie safe and sound, Joy is back safely in England, Miss Bright's found a long-lost friend, and Mr. Bright has got loads and loads of money in the bank just waiting to help Joy when she wants to go out and be a missionary again. And I think that Miss Bright and Joy ought to go and be missionaries together, and start a little school, and teach all the children about God, and then we could go out in the holidays and stay with them, and we'd be the only people in our form to go to India or Africa, or wherever it is, for our holidays. . . ."

"Here, steady on," her father said. "Don't you think you could let people organize their own lives for a change?"

"And that reminds me," Jane said, "what was it you were going to show me about Belle's bridle, Cathy? You never did tell me."

But the mystery of Belle's bridle is another story, I'm afraid!